A Tale of Three Cities

A Novel Approach to the Book of Jonah

Lewis A. Miller

Copyright © 2002 by Lewis A. Miller

A Tale of Three Cities
by Lewis A. Miller

Printed in the United States of America

Library of Congress Control Number: 2002110754
ISBN 1-591601-91-6

All rights reserved. No part of this publication may be reproduced or transmitted in any form or by any means without written permission of the publisher.

Unless otherwise indicated, Bible quotations are taken from the New International Version. Copyright © 1996 by Zondervan Corporation.

Xulon Press
11350 Random Hills Road
Suite 800
Fairfax, VA 22030
(703) 279-6511
XulonPress.com

To order additional copies, call 1-866-909-BOOK (2665).

Contents

Introduction vii
An Outline xiii
A Look at the Book xvii
I. Chapter One:
Running From God 21
   A. City #1: Nineveh, the Place of God's Will 25
   B. City #2: Tarshish, the Place of Our Own Will 29
   C. City #3: Joppa, the Place of Decision 32
   D. Everything You Have Always Wanted to Know
      about Sinking a Ship 38
II. Chapter Two:
Running To God 53
   A. Now that I'm Here, I don't Like it 54
   B. Theology Lessons from Fish Seminary 58
III. Chapter Three:
Running With God 67
   A. Why Did Revival Come to Nineveh? 69
   B. What Did Revival Bring to Nineveh? 81
IV. Chapter Four:
Running Ahead of God 87

A. An Evangelist Who Did Not Want Revival 88
B. A Graduate Degree for a Slow Learner 102
V. Chapter Five:
Personal Experiences in Nineveh 109
A. Evangelism in Nineveh 110
B. Spiritual Spectaculars in Nineveh 117
C. Laughter in Nineveh 125
D. Unusual Happenings in Nineveh 128
E. Family Life in Nineveh 130
F. Financial Freedom in Nineveh...................................132
VI. Chapter Six:
The Unwritten Last Chapter 141
Conclusion 153

INTRODUCTION

The Book of Jonah, located in the clean unused section of most Bibles, is probably the best known but least understood section of the Scriptures. Most people know about a man who was swallowed by a whale, but the book itself is often looked upon with ridicule and considered to be a fable. Sadly, many choose the story of Jonah and the whale as the prime reason that they cannot believe the Bible to be trustworthy. But the Book is not about a whale. It details a battle of wills between God and the rebellious prophet Jonah. The fish gets only three verses out of the entire narrative.

There is a bit of Jonah in each of our hearts. Jonah's idol is Jonah. He is more committed to his own concepts of God, and how God should act, than he is to God Himself. He wants to control God.

Fortunately, we are going to see that the Lord is totally committed to turning this prophet around and using him in His eternal plan.

The Scriptures Stand Approved As Read

Little time will be spent trying to determine the authenticity of the Book of Jonah. However, accepting a literal interpretation of it is imperative. The integrity of both the Scriptures and the Lord Himself are at stake, for Jesus viewed Jonah as an historical person, not a fictional character. Jesus used this story as the only sign He would give to His generation of His own death and resurrection. He also based His call to lost men on the validity of the prophet's message: *"A wicked and adulterous generation asks for a miraculous sign, but none shall be given it except the sign of the prophet Jonah. For as Jonah was three days and three nights in the belly of the great fish, so shall the son of Man be three days and three nights in the heart of the earth. The men of Nineveh will stand up at the judgment with this generation and condemn it, for they repented at the preaching of Jonah, and now one greater than Jonah is here"* (Matthew 12:39-41). In simplistic terms, if Jesus believed the account of Jonah, I can too. We are never more like the devil than when we deny the Bible, and never more like the Lord Jesus than when we wholeheartedly accept it.

Jonah is no longer being swallowed by a fish, but rather by the skeptics and critics of our day. The religious intelligensia, with their anti-supernatural bias, seem bent on denying a straightforward historical work. For some strange reason the tearing apart of the Bible is regarded as brilliant scholarship, while accepting the entire Bible without reservation suggests naiveté, or just plain stupidity. The renowned Charles Haddon Spurgeon had a

Introduction

different take on God's Word: "There are some men who think themselves wise enough to take part of the Bible as true and discard the rest as false, but I'm not wise enough to do that. I must accept it all as God's Word, or I can't be sure of a single sentence."

Some scholars even delight in arguing that Jonah did not write the Book of Jonah. While listening to their silly arguments, we can profit from the wisdom of Mark Twain: "Shakespeare did not write Shakespeare's works, but they were written by another man with the same name." Reading Jonah's story through his own eyes makes the book come alive. Who else could have written so vividly of these experiences?

As a young man I was told by my seminary professor that the story of Jonah was a myth. He explained that such events never really happened. About the same time I heard a young evangelist, Billy Graham, say that he would believe the Bible if it said that Jonah swallowed the whale. What a dilemma! Should I believe the learned professor, or should I accept Dr. Graham's position? Choosing to agree with Billy has allowed me to live happily ever after!

Much confusion exists about the inspiration of the Scriptures. The human writers were not inspired in the same way as were many famous literary geniuses. True, they were "moved by the Holy Spirit," but inspiration is claimed for the writings, not the writers. The Scriptures themselves were *"God-breathed"* (II Timothy 3:16). While serving as a trustee of the Foreign Mission Board of the Southern Baptist Convention, I had the privilege of interviewing hundreds of candidates for overseas missions.

In stating their doctrinal views, a large majority would testify that the Bible was written by "men inspired by God." This always bothered me. The Bible does not make such a claim. Certainly the human writers spoke from God "as they were carried along by the Holy Spirit" (II Peter 1:21), but the claim for inspiration involves the finished product, not the human authors. We have an absolutely trustworthy book, the Word of God, and Jonah is a part of it. Believing the Book of Jonah, or any other Scriptures, should create no problem for a Spirit-filled believer.

The Fish Is Not the Hero

The New Testament teaches that the dominant theme of the Old Testament prophets is the Son of God. *"All the prophets testified about Him that everyone who believes in Him receives forgiveness of sins through His Name" (Acts 10:43).* Sad to say, in the Book of Jonah the fish often steals the limelight from the one who deserves the preeminence, the loving Sovereign Lord who rules over nature, nations, and individuals. The narrative reveals the lengths to which God goes to make His children obedient—and how prone we are to rebel against Him. When we focus on the loving Heavenly Father rather than on Jonah or the fish, we can joyfully sing "Great is Thy Faithfulness." (A companion song, "Great is Our Pigheadedness," would emphasize the two major themes of the Book, God's faithfulness and our stubbornness)

The well-known British preacher, G. Campbell Morgan, said "Men have been looking so hard at the great fish that

Introduction

they have failed to see the great God." The book features the Sovereign Lord and the message proclaims His love and concern for all people—not just Israelites, not just Americans, not just Baptists or Methodists. The Book of Jonah pictures a love beautiful enough to overshadow the ugly picture of Jonah, and all of us who are so much like him.

AN OUTLINE

*P*lainly, this writing is not an attempt at a scholarly work. While I have long since forgotten the Hebrew and Greek that I learned in my years of seminary study, I have never forgotten the many verses that I memorized during my first few years as a believer. Simple Bible truths that I learned in personal study have meant far more to me and to my ministry than all my formal classroom education.

The controversial Dr. J. Frank Norris furnishes some support for my lack of scholarly dignity. In the preface of "Lectures on Isaiah," Dr. Norris wrote in the 1930's: "The notes and outlines of this volume will, no doubt, meet with severe criticism of the scholars, but since the scholars represent only about 1/1,000 of 1% of the population, according to census, or, rather since 999/1,000 of the two billion humans make up the ordinary rank and file, these notes have been prepared to help the sincere, honest, Mr. Everyday, plain citizen and humble Christian."

The "sincere, honest Mr. Everyday" means people like

my twelve grandkids. Let the skeptical scholars indulge in their pseudo-intellectual debates about who wrote Jonah, whether he actually existed, the existential value of whale-blubber, and perhaps who was mayor of Nineveh at the time. It doesn't matter to me if my grandkids ever achieve such theological "brilliance." I want only for each of them to know the Sovereign Lord Jesus personally, and to grow spiritually by profiting from the mistakes of both Jonah and their grandpa. I dedicate this book to each of them.

A familiar outline, author unknown, has been passed down through the decades:

> Chapter One: Running *from* God
> Chapter Two: Running *to* God
> Chapter Three: Running *with* God
> Chapter Four: Running *ahead of* God

Launching out from this outline, the plan for our study centers around the three cities mentioned in the Book of Jonah—Nineveh, Tarshish, and Joppa. Our concern is not to study the historical account of Jonah's travels to these cities, nor are we interested in a geographical study. Instead, we will view these three cities as personal illustrations of spiritual life.

First, Nineveh, the place where God desired Jonah to be, will represent His will for our lives—not the far-off, ancient, heathen city. To get to your Nineveh, you may not even need to move from your seat. Faithfulness to God and living in the center of His will are that matters.

Secondly, Tarshish, where Jonah desired to be,

An Outline

represents our human will and the attitude, "I'll do it my way." Life in Tarshish can usually be depicted as a desire for material prosperity and an attractive comfort zone. In ancient times, the Tarshish navy carried "gold, silver, ivory, apes, and peacocks" (I Kings 10:22), all of which suggests luxurious living.

Thirdly, Joppa, where Jonah decided to flee from the presence of the Lord, represents the place of spiritual decision: "Will I let Jesus be the Lord of my life (Nineveh), or will I do my own thing (Tarshish)?"

I realize that Jonah never made it to Tarshish. I am also aware that Nineveh was destroyed in ancient times because of its wickedness. Nevertheless, I believe that there is an important life-changing message for believers who apply this three-city allegory to their Christian lives.

So, if you are one of those "rank and file, sincere, everyday, plain citizens, "A Tale of Three Cities" is written for you. May the Lord empower and enable you to make the right spiritual choices so that you can live in "downtown Nineveh," right in the center of His will.

A LOOK AT THE BOOK

Jonah was a prophet in Israel. His name in Hebrew means "dove," while the name of his father, Amittai, means "truth." His hometown, Gath-hepher, was about four miles from Jesus' hometown of Nazareth. While the Book of Jonah pictures him as a disobedient man who wanted his own way, Jonah wasn't always rebellious. At one time he was a faithful prophet: *"He [King Jereboam] was the one who restored the boundaries of Israel from Lebo Hamath to the Sea of Arabah, in accordance with the Word of the Lord, the God of Israel, spoken through his servant Jonah son of Amittai, the prophet from Gath Hepher" (II Kings 14:25).*

While the prophet Amos was commissioned by God to deliver the news of impending destruction, Jonah had the more pleasant assignment of telling King Jeroboam that God was going to deliver His people from the Syrians. On the basis of Jonah's message, Jeroboam got his army together and defeated the enemy. For the first time in 150 years, the borders of Israel were realigned to where they had been in David and Solomon's time. Jonah was delighted. Being a prophet was fun, as long as God wanted what Jonah wanted. He enjoyed delivering good news. Let men like Amos handle the tough stuff.

As the years passed, however, God presented a new ministry to Jonah. Now he was directed to preach in the great city of Nineveh. The assignment turned the prophet into a renegade against God. While the Lord ordered him to go about 600 miles to the northeast, Jonah decided to go about 1400 miles west, to what he thought was the end of the world, a sure hiding-place from God.

Jonah's distaste for this mission was understandable. Nineveh was the largest city in the rising Assyrian Empire. She already had a reputation for military strength and unspeakable barbarianism. Jonah, a loyal and patriotic Jew, wanted nothing to do with leading Israel's strongest enemy to repentance and forgiveness. The Assyrians were bitter foes who deserved judgment, and Jonah was quite content with the prospect of their destruction.

Not long after his attempt *"to flee from the presence of the Lord,"* Jonah realized his folly. After clearing port in Joppa, the ship carrying the rebellious prophet was suddenly imperiled by a violent storm which did not subside until Jonah was thrown overboard. Instead of drowning, Jonah found refuge in a great fish that God had prepared for the occasion (1:4-17).

Through this harrowing experience, God brought His prophet to a place of submission. From inside the fish Jonah uttered a prayer of praise, thanksgiving, and total dedication.

When the Lord spoke to the fish, Jonah was vomited onto dry land (2:1-10).

God renewed His missionary commission to Jonah. This time the prophet was ready to obey. He entered Nineveh and faithfully, though reluctantly, preached the message God had given him: *"Forty more days and Nineveh will be destroyed."* The pagan people immediately believed what the prodigal prophet proclaimed. Even the king repented. He sent out a proclamation that all people should pray and turn from their evil ways. In return, God changed His heart toward the people and spared the city in what might well be the greatest revival in human history (3:1-10).

Instead of being delighted with his role in this great missionary endeavor, Jonah was so displeased with Nineveh's reprieve that he prayed for God to take his life. As he sat pouting outside the city, still hoping to see God's judgment fall, God used a series of object lessons—a gourd, a worm, and an east wind—all designed to bring Jonah to the end of himself (4:1-11).

It seems likely that Jonah later confessed his sins and was privileged to write this account for us. As for the wicked city, the repentant attitude of the people averted God's judgment for about one hundred fifty years.

Jesus used this story of Jonah to foretell His own death and resurrection to the scribes and Pharisees: *"For as Jonah was a sign to the Ninevites, so also will the Son of Man be to this generation." (Luke 11:29-30).* Just as Jonah departed from the fish after three days and three nights, so too, the crucified Christ left the tomb in the same time frame.

A Tale of Three Cities

Many centuries after Jonah had concluded his ministry, Simon Peter wrote of Jesus: *"We are witnesses of everything He did in the country of the Jews and in Jerusalem. They killed Him by hanging Him on a tree, but God raised Him from the dead on the third day and caused Him to be seen...He commanded us to preach to the people and to testify that He is the one whom God appointed as judge of the living and the dead. All the prophets testify about Him that everyone who believes in Him receives forgiveness of sins through His name"* (Acts 10:39-40,42-43).

CHAPTER ONE

RUNNING FROM GOD

"*The word of God came to Jonah son of Amittai: 'Go to the great city of Nineveh and preach against it, because its wickedness has come up before me.' But Jonah ran away from the Lord and headed for Tarshish. He went down to Joppa, where he found a ship bound for that port. After paying the fare, he went aboard and sailed for Tarshish to flee from the Lord"* (1:1-3).

Something new was in store for Jonah. The Lord called him by name, indicating that He had a special assignment for His prophet, just as He has for each of His children. When He saves us, God has more on His mind than "heaven someday." Each believer becomes a minister, saved to serve others and to make a wholesome mark on this world.

The prophet was not asked *if* he wanted to go to Nineveh.

A Tale of Three Cities

There was no need for Jonah to prayerfully consider this matter. The Sovereign Lord gave him directions, and Jonah's only responsibility was to obey. Today, in like fashion, the Lord Jesus gives each member of His body spiritual gifts and corresponding ministries. As the Head of the church, He commissions us to carry the Gospel to the entire world. Our only response is to obey the particular orders He gives.

God left nothing to chance in Jonah's call—not the minister, the ministry, the message, the place, or the time. "Jonah—I want you—to go—preach—repentance—in Nineveh—now." Everything God wanted was clearly spelled out. God didn't play "I've Got a Secret" in directing Jonah. He doesn't keep His children guessing about His will, and Jonah did not have to flip a coin to determine what God wanted him to do. Jonah knew clearly the will of God. He knew it, but He blew it!

Jonah could think of much better things to do than to serve his nation's worst enemy. With his intense spirit of Jewish patriotism and the resulting prejudices, we can almost hear him saying, "Nineveh? Really, God, You've got to be kidding." Jonah's hatred was rooted in racial prejudice, religious bigotry, and cultural exclusivity of the worst kind.

Dr. Donald Grey Barnhouse once compared Jonah's call to Nineveh with asking a Jew from New York to go to Hitler during World War II to tell him that God loved him and would forgive him if he would repent. Instead, the Jew hops a train headed for San Francisco, then boards a ship bound for Japan. "No, thank you" to such an absurd assignment.

God did not call Jonah to Nineveh in order to get a sadistic thrill from the prophet's pain and frustration.

Christians sometimes have a perverse idea that the Heavenly Father delights in sending us to places we don't like. Not so! The believers' promise is that if we delight ourselves in the Lord, He gives us the desires of our hearts (Psalm 37:4). However, the Lord always knows what is right for us, and we only think we know. His assignments often show a compassion for the people to whom we minister and character development for us as well. Willing obedience to the Lord would have made Nineveh the most blessed spot in the world for Jonah, even better than living at home in downtown Jerusalem.

Jonah evidently needed a new perspective of God. The delight of his past ministry was gone. His own opinions, perhaps strengthened with support from other biased Jews, kept him from seeing an ever-faithful and loving God. And, at this point, the farthest thing from Jonah's mind was the character development of a rusted-out servant.

I Don't Want Nineveh to Get Under My Skin

Why would God be concerned about Nineveh? Here was the world's largest city with a population estimated between 600,000 and 1,000,000. Located in what today is known as Northern Iraq, this splendid city was so full of wickedness, violence, and cruelty that it defies our imagination. The stench of Nineveh's sins had reached the nostrils of God (1:2).

Men saw only the culture and wealth of Nineveh, but God's holy eyes saw a city bent on destruction. Violence was the national sin. One of their legendary kings wrote about his conquest: "I stormed the mountain peaks and took them. In the midst of the mighty mountain I slaughtered them, with their blood I dyed the mountain red like wool. With the rest of them I darkened the gullies and precipices of the mountains. I carried off their possessions. The heads of their warriors I cut off, and I formed them into a pillar over against their city, their young men and their maidens I burned in the fire." Assyrian soldiers were known for skinning captives alive. (No wonder Jonah didn't want to let them get under his skin!) To a Jewish prophet it might seem that the God of Israel should not care at all about such sinful people.

Assyria was Israel's arch enemy. When Jonah heard God's warning about overthrowing Nineveh, he undoubtedly responded with "Yippee." Assyria's destruction could only be a dream-come-true for any loyal Jew. So why be bothered about it? Why warn the enemy? Why give them a chance to change? Let them continue in their sinful ways so that the Lord would carry out His plans to extinguish the whole city.

After his eventual arrival in Nineveh, Jonah explained his resistance to traveling there. He prayed: *"O Lord, is this not what I said when I was still at home? That is why I was so quick to flee to Tarshish. I knew that you are a gracious and compassionate God, slow to anger and abounding in love, a God who relents from sending calamity" (4:2)*. At the end of three chapters (and a fish ride), Jonah had not changed much.

"A Tale of Three Cities" explores the Sovereign Lord's hand at work. Each of the three locations—Nineveh, Tarshish and Joppa—represent various phases of our spiritual walk. The principles which God used in guiding Jonah can be extremely beneficial when applied to our lives.

A. CITY #1:

NINEVEH, THE PLACE OF GOD'S WILL

Each believer has a personal Nineveh, the place where we die to everything except God's will. In Nineveh we ally ourselves totally with God. Personal ambitions and reputations are set aside so that Jesus Christ can be given His rightful place of preeminence.

The Lord frequently shared the "Nineveh Principle" with His apostles. He said, *"If anyone should come after me, he must deny himself and take up his cross and follow me. For whoever wants to save his life will lose it, but whoever loses his life for me and for the gospel will save it" (Mark 8:34-35).*

Finding Life by Losing It

Spiritual teachings have no appeal to our natural minds: *"The man without the Spirit does not accept the things that come from the Spirit of God, for they are foolishness to him, and he cannot understand them, because they are spiritually discerned" (I Corinthians 2:14).* The Nineveh Principle (that is, the Jesus Principle) is frowned upon and ridiculed in almost every classroom of almost every institution in our land, including some seminaries. Consider what is being said. The secret to living is dying, getting self out of the way so Jesus can live in us. It sounds almost morbid. Our pride and our spiritual stubbornness rebel against this way of life, preventing us from sharing God's victory. There seems to be a lot of Jonah in all of us.

Nineveh-living can be summed up in one word—*obedience.* The Nineveh lifestyle is best described in Paul's testimony: *"I am crucified with Christ; nevertheless I live; yet not I, but Christ lives in me, and the life I now live in the flesh I live by the faith of the Son of God, who loved me and gave himself for me" (Galatians 2:20 KJV).*

I Can't—The First Step to Victory

God used those two little words, *"Not I,"* to significantly change my life sixteen years after my conversion. While I was serving on a foreign mission field, the Lord used a ministry failure to teach me that "the Christian life is not hard to live; it is impossible." I learned in very practical ways that the theme for all valid Christian living is, "Not I, but Christ lives in me." No matter how hard I try, or no matter what religious duties I perform, I can't master the Christian life any better than I could save myself. Thankfully, the Lord Jesus Christ offered to both save me and live in me.

Only Christ Can Live the Christian Life

The Christian life can usually be divided into four phases: First, it's *easy.* At the time of conversion our ecstatic emotions cause us to rejoice in our new life. For days, weeks, even months, we are on a "spiritual high." Then, moving into the second stage, life becomes *difficult* as we realize the demands the Lord makes on us. We come back down to earth from Cloud Nine. We discover the hardships involved in the new life of a believer. Next comes the *impossible* third stage in which we admit (if only to ourselves) that we can not live up to Christian standards. This is what Paul meant when he said, *"Not I."* We often find ourselves going through acceptable church-prescribed motions, but nothing seems to really work. This third stage is the crucial point in a Christian's life. Many "throw in the towel" and quit, just short of the thrilling victory stage.

If a believer acknowledges the reality of "Not I," spiritual excitement will follow. *"Not I"* changes to *"but Christ lives in me,"* and we enter the fourth stage—*the obedient life* in downtown Nineveh. Throughout the first three stages God has been challenging us to submit to Lordship, letting Jesus be Boss. He must bring us to the end of the Tarshish self-life, so that Jesus can live His life in and through us. His life becomes my spiritual victory in the most practical issues I face.

Believers experience progressive victory while living in Nineveh. Here, *"we walk by faith, not by sight" (II Corinthians 5:7)*. This means living without scheming, without manipulating others to accomplish my own desires. Living in Nineveh means that we must give God the only thing He ever asked for—our bodies as living sacrifices. Only in Nineveh can we ever know *"what is that good and acceptable and perfect will of God"* (*Romans 12:1-2*). Spiritual decisions become more than guesses or coin-tosses when Jesus is Lord. Trusting in the Lord with all our hearts and leaning not on our own understanding brings His direction to our lives. (*Proverbs 3:5-6*).

Extremely Valuable "Nothings"

The first principle of life in Nineveh is a tough one. We must accept God's evaluation of us, and it isn't pleasant. Certainly He loves us, but at the same time He realizes that without Him we are spiritual "nothings." Paul wrote: *"If anyone thinks he is something when he is nothing, he deceives himself" (Galatians 6:3)*. How deceived we are to think that we can build self-esteem using the world's criteria—material possessions, good looks, education, and over-achievement! Paul, perhaps the most spiritual man who ever lived, testified *"though I be nothing" (II Corinthians 12:11)*. And the Lord's evaluation of our works doesn't help to build up our egos either: *"for without me you can do nothing" (John 15:5)*.

But what does this do to our self-esteem? In Nineveh we don't need it! We have Christ-esteem. We are children of the King. And the King lives in us! What sweet relief not to have to establish our own worth! God the Father loved me since eternity past! God the Son purchased my salvation two thousand years ago! God the Holy Spirit lives in me and never forsakes me. No need to play politics, or to " know the right people," or to have to "look out for Number One." Nineveh-living is exciting because it is *"not I, but Christ."* Nothings though we may be, our lives are worthwhile, full of holy excitement. Like Paul we can say: *"I can do everything through him who gives me strength" (Philippians 4:13)*.

Making the Invisible Christ Visible

When Jesus is experienced as Lord, we exert a wholesome influence on those around us. Peter wrote: *"In your hearts set apart Christ as Lord. Always be prepared to give an answer to everyone who asks you to give the reason for the hope that you have" (I Peter 3:15).* Godly believers always make an impact on others.

A pastor's enemies hired a detective to "get the goods on him," so that they could fire him. Thirteen weeks after the surveillance began, the detective came to the pastor and said, "After watching your life for the past three months, I am sick of my sinful life. I want to know your Jesus." Though he realized that he might lose his job and his license, the detective received Jesus as the Lord and Savior of his life. Where did this pastor live? It is obvious—downtown Nineveh! Spirit-filled believers make the invisible Christ visible!

B. CITY #2

TARSHISH, THE PLACE OF OUR OWN WILL

For Jonah, it was Tarshish or bust! He wanted his own way at any cost, and the cost was unbelievably high! In Tarshish, a child of God does his own thing. Money, popularity, peer pressure, and selfish pursuits all mean more than pleasing the Lord. It is a lifestyle of pushing and promoting self, developing a feeling of self-worth, getting to know the right people, and merely going through the motions of living the Christian life. The Scriptures best summarize Tarshish-living: *"The backslider in heart shall be filled with his own ways"* (Proverbs 14:14 KJV).

The Tarshish-life is full of frustration and pressure. Carnal believers have to look out for the "Big I." This means constantly competing with everyone, walking over peers to achieve goals, buying friends, and compromising spiritual convictions so we can please others. Anything done by Tarshish residents in the name of Christ is fakery, designed simply to make us look good.

No true believer can really enjoy life in Tarshish. It is a place of total discontentment, where believers are spiritually desensitized and hardened to spiritual truth.

Go East, Young Man

Many scholars believe Lisbon, Portugal, to be the modern site of Tarshish. Others believe it to be a Phoenician seaport in Spain (Genesis 10:4; Isaiah 23:1). Wherever it was, Tarshish was believed in Jonah's day to be the farthest point west, the end of the world. Just beyond Tarshish were the "Gates of Hercules," known today as Gibraltar. Out beyond that, a ship would drop off into nothing. We can say then that Jonah tried to go to the end of the world, about 1400 miles westward, to get away from God's assignment. Jonah's only desire was to *"flee from the presence of the Lord."*

The Way of the Transgressor Is Hard

Jonah soon discovered that running from God brings misery. Centuries later, when the apostle Paul attempted to live in his own way, he testified: *"What a wretched man I am! Who will rescue me from this body of death?" (Romans 7:24).* Nineveh-living is certainly not easy, but there the Lord provides a support system of joy and peace, so we can enthusiastically sing "Victory in Jesus." The Lord said to some dedicated believers: *"In this world you will have trouble. But take heart! I have overcome the world"* (John 16:33).

By contrast, a Christian in Tarshish (or even on the way there) feels like a battlefield. The indwelling Holy Spirit works overtime to bring true believers to the end of self. The flesh wars against the Spirit. Satan usually sees to it that Tarshish-dwellers prosper financially and materially, but they can never know real spiritual prosperity. Chances are even good that a believer may win the lottery! Job promotions may come quickly, but they fail to produce any real joy. Life is hectic.

Tarshish is a ratrace that the Lord never intended for His children. The believer conforms to the desires of his peers, and the will of God means little or nothing. Family life usually becomes extremely messy. The pursuit of happiness produces emptiness. The believer in Tarshish may play church games, but the Lord doesn't seem real. No true heartfelt devotion is exercised toward Him. Life in Tarshish is the pits!

Tarshish is also characterized by such hideous sins as self-pity, scheming, manipulating others, and never accepting blame for anything. Just as Eve in the "Garden of Tarshish" blamed Adam, and Adam blamed the serpent, we never want to face the truth about ourselves when we are "out-of-sorts" with the Lord. Humanistic psychologists have had a field day teaching guilty sinners to blame their problems on their parents, their awful childhood days, their environment, anything other than the real problem. Certainly child abuse is despicable, even diabolical, and should be punished, but parents should not usually be blamed for the failures of their Christian children. When we are born again, we get a new Father, and He can overrule all the past situations, even those caused by less-than-worthwhile earthly parents. *"Therefore, if anyone is in Christ, he is a new creation; the old has gone, the new has come" (II Corinthians 5:17).* So, it's you—not your parents, your teachers, your boss, or your friends—standing in need of prayer. Accept full blame for your Tarshish existence, then *"cast all your anxiety on him, because he cares for you" (I Peter 5:7)*

C. CITY #3

JOPPA, THE PLACE OF DECISION

Joppa, known today as Jaffa, is the port where Jonah made the decision which influenced his life. This city represents the place where each believer decides either to obey God in Nineveh or to set sail for Tarshish to do his own thing.

Verses, Not Voices or Visions

"But Jonah ran away from the Lord and headed for Tarshish. He went down to Joppa, where he found a ship bound for that port. After paying the fare, he went aboard and sailed for Tarshish to flee from the Lord" (1:3).

Do not be surprised when doors open for a journey to Tarshish. Sin usually starts easy, and the devil often provides a convenient ship for runaways. Circumstances, if they are to reveal the will of God to us, must always be in harmony with the Word of God and the leading of the Spirit of God. We are not to be guided primarily by "open doors," but by open Bibles. When we open the scriptures, God opens His mouth! The psalmist said, *"Your Word is a lamp unto my feet and a light for my path" (Psalm 119:105).* Jonah had no trouble starting his journey away from the Lord. The Joppa Travel Agency just happened to have a Tarshish-bound ship in port, and Jonah had just enough money to pay his fare! How convenient! All the doors were opened, but obviously the Lord had not opened them.

God Speaks the Last Word

"Then the Lord sent a great wind on the sea, and such a violent storm arose that the ship threatened to break up" (1:4).

The first two words of verse three furnish us with perhaps the best definition of sin in the entire Bible. Jonah was not what we would call a "bad man." His lifestyle shows no trace of adultery, drunkenness, or dishonesty. Until politics became more important to him than obedience, he had been a faithful prophet of God. *"But Jonah"* was the problem These words reveal a heart full of rebellion against the Sovereign Lord. Instead of walking with God, Jonah was now running from Him. *"But Jonah"* leads to Tarshish. Of course, Jonah never really got there, but even sailing in that direction showed the misery of being out of God's will. A Joppa-to-Tarshish journey usually took about two years, but Jonah probably thought such a long cruise would do him good. What better way to put God out of his mind and escape from His presence! *"But the Lord"* (1:4) is in direct contrast with the previous verse, *"But Jonah."* God speaks the last word in every life. *"But the Lord sent a great wind on the sea, and a violent storm arose."* Neither Jonah, nor any of us, can thwart the plan and purpose of the Almighty God.

To Which Place Does God Address Your Mail?

Joppa is the place of decision for those who have already received Jesus Christ. Having been born spiritually, the believer must now choose either a life of obedience to his Lord (Nineveh) or the self-directed life (Tarshish). The choice involves living in the power of the Spirit (Nineveh) or trusting in the power of the flesh (Tarshish). Believers can either struggle to do their best (Tarshish) or yield to let Christ do *His* best in them (Nineveh).

Well, I Reckon So

Death to self is the only passport to residency in Nineveh. But a word of caution! This is not a do-it-yourself job. Many Christians have attempted, with disastrous results, to crucify themselves. Self-crucifixion is impossible. Symbolically you can make a cross, lie on it, put nails through your feet and one hand, but that is as far as you will get. You are not commanded to crucify yourself. What is commanded is *reckoning*, acting on what God says is true. The Biblical principle of death to self is an accomplished fact. In God's sight every blood-bought, born-again child has *already* been crucified and resurrected with Christ. Since the Bible says this is true, we must act on it. That's what reckoning means. It doesn't matter whether we understand it or feel like it. God's Word says that we have been crucified with Christ and also made alive in Him.

A Lot of Dying that Day

Paul laid down some hard-to-accept principles for us: *"For we know that our old self was crucified with him so that the body of sin might be rendered powerless, that we should no longer be slaves to sin"(Romans 6:8)*. Then reckoning takes place: *"In the same way, count ('reckon'—KJV) yourselves dead to sin but alive to God in Christ Jesus" (Romans 6:11)*.

When did our self-crucifixion take place? At Calvary with Jesus! That's what Paul meant when he said, *"I have been crucified with Christ"* (Galatians 2:20). In God's eyes, we were in Jesus that day—the very reason He punished His sinless Son. *"He himself bore our sins in his body on the* tree, so that we might die to sins and live for righteousness; by his wounds you have been healed" (I Peter 2:24). With natural vision, we can see only three crosses, but God saw His Son, two thieves, Paul, me, you, and all the sinners of the world dying on that middle cross. Whatever happened to Jesus (death, burial, and resurrection) happened to every believer—in God's sight! When we reckon ourselves *"dead to sin, but alive to God in Christ Jesus"* (Romans 6:11), God's moving van pulls up to our doorstep in Tarshish, and we are Nineveh-bound! When we reckon ourselves to be dead to sin, Christ begins to live His beautiful life in us.

But be careful! Note that sin did not die to us. Regretfully we must acknowledge that sin is still quite alive. Sin has not separated itself from us, but we believers are dead to sin. This simply means that we do not have to *serve* sin any longer: *"For sin shall not be your master, because you are not under law, but under grace"* (Romans 6:14).

"Hang It on Your Beak, Boss"

While in seminary I worked in an ice plant for the meanest man in town. I was in slavery to O. B. because he was my boss. Working under such conditions can make life unbearable. The icehouse always chilled when O. B. showed up. I had to put up with a lot to earn $1.10 an hour. If I finished my assigned office work early, he would order me to stack 300 pound blocks of ice (fortunately they slid!), or crack the ice, or clean the dock—anything to make me miserable! When he said, "Miller, chop the ice," I chopped the ice. When he commanded me to clean the dock, I cleaned the dock, even though these tasks were not in my job description. Finally, I got a pastorate and was able to quit my job at the ice plant. Several years later I visited my former co-workers there. Our joyful reunion was interrupted by O.B.'s arrival. But something was different! O. B. was still alive, but he had no control or dominion over me. If he had yelled, "Miller, chop some ice," or "clean the dock," my polite reply would have been, "O. B., hang it on your beak!" O. B. was still the powerful boss of the ice plant, but he was not *my* boss. I had been set free from him. He was not dead, but I was "dead to him." No longer did he have any control over me.

"Hang It on Your Beak, Sin"

Did I say that O. B. was the worst boss I ever had? Wrong! Sin was a far more horrible boss. I served this cruel, life-wrecking taskmaster for twenty-three long years. Then one day I met Jesus, *"in whom we have redemption through his blood, the forgiveness of sins, in accordance with the riches of God's grace"* (Ephesians 1:7). I received Him, not merely as Savior, but as the new Lord of my life. He replaced sin as my boss. Like O. B., sin is still alive, a dominant force in the world. And sin still makes strong demands on me, but now I can stand up and say, "Sin, you are not my boss any longer. I am a child of the King! Jesus is my new Boss, so I'm not going to let you mess me up anymore." This is called *reckoning*. This is death to self.

Tarshish-living is foolish. It's like visiting the ice plant and allowing old O. B. to continue to boss me around. It is acknowledging that sin is a better boss and can do a better job of running my life than Jesus can. I don't need sin's domination anymore. I have a new Boss, my wonderful Lord!

The Worker Is More Important than the Work

How God loves His children! He actually seemed to be more concerned about straightening out one prodigal prophet than He was about dealing with the world's largest city. At any rate, He delayed His ministry to the city while He worked on His runaway child. God emphasizes the worth of each individual. He is more concerned about you than about any assignment He has given you. He is more concerned with what you *are* than what you *do*. He always puts people ahead of programs. He withheld revival from Nineveh for a season until He could persuade His reluctant prophet to move there.

D. EVERYTHING YOU HAVE ALWAYS WANTED TO KNOW ABOUT SINKING A SHIP

Jonah didn't write Psalm 139, but he certainly learned the truth expressed by the Psalmist: *"—Where can I go from your Spirit? Where can I flee from your presence? If I go up to the heavens, you are there; if I make my bed in the depths, you are there. If I rise on the wings of the dawn, if I settle on the far side of the sea, even there your hand will guide me, your right hand will hold me fast"* (Ps. 139:7-10).

Jonah's folly led him to an interesting series of

educational pursuits—first aboard ship, then in the sea, and finally three days in "Fish College." Although it is usually true that "the only thing we learn from history is that we never learn anything from history," several life-changing challenges are set before us.

Lesson 1:
You cannot run from God by
merely changing your address.

Paul wrote: *"Each one should remain in the situation which he was in when God called him" (I Corinthians 7:20).* In other words, *stay put!* Assume that you are where God wants you now, doing what He desires, living in the very circumstances He has designed for you at this moment. Then promise never to move *until He moves you.* Obeying this principle avoids many heartaches and eliminates countless hours trying to determine His will. The Lord will always make it crystal clear when He wants you to make a change. In the meantime, stay where you are, and do not even think of changing your situation.

The average American moves once every four years, and the average pastor moves about every two years. Often this moving is just an attempt to change ugly circumstances. For Christians out of fellowship with God, restlessness promotes a lifestyle of making changes. Hopping from one situation to another—new jobs, new homes, new mates, or new churches—often indicates a lack of inner peace. The grass may seem greener on the other side, but it often turns out to be Astroturf.

"We Have Met the Enemy, and He Is Us"

When the Holy Spirit is quenched in a Christian's life, the victim will always seek new places, new people, and new toys. Tarshish-living is usually characterized by discontentment and confusion. God doesn't provide rest and peace in Tarshish, or even on the way there. He never wants His people getting comfortable away from Nineveh. Constant jumping from one situation to another in Tarshish never helps, because the real problem always abides. In Tarshish, you ARE the problem. Of course, you blame your mate, your parents, your kids, your boss, your pastor, your cat (probably a part of the problem!), or your best friend. The real problem, however, is the civil war raging inside you, the flesh warring against the spirit. The eminent philosopher, Pogo, summed it up beautifully: "We have met the enemy, and he is us!"

Paul wrote: *"I have learned to be content whatever the circumstances"* *(Philippians 4:11)*. Remember though that Paul was in the downtown Nineveh stage of his life, not in Tarshish, when he wrote this. The only safe and wise move for a Tarshish-dweller is the one that takes him to downtown Nineveh.

Moving from one situation to another in Tarshish merely puts the same miseries in a new environment. God knows what is best for His children, and He wants us to experience His best. As long as we move about in Tarshish trying to gratify the flesh, self is in control. The spiritual freshness and delight which we seek eludes us.

A move to Nineveh acknowledges Jesus as our personal

Boss. We do not even *make* Him Lord; God has already done that. Peter preached: *"Therefore, let all Israel be assured of this: God has made this Jesus, whom you crucified, both Lord and Christ" (Acts 2:36).* We simply acknowledge His Lordship by responding to Calvary with the presentation of our bodies as living sacrifices, a total surrender. *"Trust in the Lord with all your heart and lean not on your own understanding; in all your ways acknowledge Him and He will direct your paths" (Proverbs 3:5-6 KJV).*

Lesson 2:
A storm always appears
when we try to outwit God.

"But Jonah ran away from the Lord and headed for Tarshish. He went down to Joppa, where he found a ship bound for that port. After paying the fare, he went aboard and sailed for Tarshish to flee from the Lord. Then the Lord sent a great wind on the sea, and such a violent storm arose that the ship threatened to break up. All the sailors were afraid and each cried out to his own god. And they threw the cargo into the sea to lighten the ship. But Jonah had gone below deck, where he lay down and fell into a deep sleep" (1:3-6).

Jonah boarded a ship that was crossing the Mediterranean during the storm season. That wasn't very bright of the prophet, but nothing is bright about trying to run away from God. Even the seasoned veterans of the ocean knew though that this was not an ordinary storm but one that was supernatural in its origin.

The Fugitive

While on our honeymoon many years ago, Joanna and I visited a large church on Sunday evening. After the service, our conversation with a deacon was interrupted by a tramp requesting a handout. The poor, dirty soul in tattered clothes looked like death-warmed-over. As the deacon left to make provision for the man's needs, I began to share with Him about the Lord Jesus. I soon learned though that he was well-grounded in the Scriptures, for he joined with me to finish quoting every verse I used. Then he asked: "Son, would you be surprised to know that I have been born again?" When I responded that I would, he testified that he had been saved many years before and was a graduate of a highly respected Bible institute.

This wasted little man told of making several recent attempts to take his own life, offering two fresh deep gashes on his wrists as evidence. I have never forgotten his testimony: "This is what resulted when the Lord said, 'Africa' (spelled N-i-n-e-v-e-h), but I said, 'No, Cincinnati' (T-a-r-s-h-i-s-h)."

This rebellious runaway was guilty of nothing more than building a mission church in Cincinnati when the Lord wanted him in Africa. Years later, a fellow graduate of his school told me that the work in Cincinnati had prospered until the disobedient pastor suddenly faltered. This preacher bore the scars of a religious Tarshish-dweller who tried to outwit God.

"Be not deceived: God cannot be mocked. A man reaps what he sows. The one who sows to please his sinful nature, from that nature will reap destruction [Paraphrase: The one

who sows to Tarshish will reap Tarshish-destruction]; *the one who sows to please the Spirit, from the Spirit will reap eternal life* [The one who sows to Nineveh will reap Nineveh benefits]" *(Galatians 6:7-8).*

**Lesson 3:
The course of sin is always downward.**

Perhaps it is just a play on words, but Jonah went *down* to Joppa (1:3), *down* below the deck of the ship (1:5), *down* to the sea (1:15), and *down* into the fish's belly (1:17). What we can safely say is that when we are Tarshish-bound, the course is always downward. The devil furnishes a greasy slide for us. For the man who tries to escape God, every step is down. His joy goes, his power goes, his communion with God goes, his liberty goes. Everything he thought worthwhile is gone. Perhaps worst of all, the downward spiral caused by our disobedience seizes others and pulls them down with us.

Tarshish is often a place of material and financial success: *"For the king had at sea a navy of Tarshish with the navy of Hiram; once in three years came the navy of Tarshish, bringing gold, and silver, ivory, and apes, and peacocks" (I Kings 10:22).* The devil allows backsliders to grow materially prosperous, but there is no accompanying peace. Even promotions turn out to be demotions. Tarshish money may buy many things, but these things do not bring joy. The riches fade, and life becomes empty.

Most inhabitants of Tarshish live to get rich, the most dangerous goal a person can have! Making big money is certainly the number one idol in our country today. What a scary promise God makes to anyone, rich or poor, whose life commitment is to become wealthy. *"People who want to get rich fall into temptation and a trap and into many foolish and harmful desires that plunge men into ruin and destruction. For the love of money is a root of all kinds of evil. Some people, eager for money, have wandered from the faith and pierced themselves with many griefs" (I Timothy 6:9-10).* What a stern warning against letting money draw us to Tarshish. Woe to the one whose goal in life is to get rich!

God provides only a downward path of despair and frustration in Tarshish. All of His promised blessings are addressed to those living in downtown Nineveh!

Lesson 4:
A Christian in sin is the most dangerous man alive.

Then the sailors said to each other, 'Come, let us cast lots to find out who is responsible for this calamity.' They cast lots and the lot fell on Jonah. So they asked him, 'Tell us, who is responsible for making all this trouble for us? What do you do? Where do you come from? What is your country? From what people are you?' He answered, 'I am a Hebrew and I worship the Lord, the God of heaven, who made the sea and the land.' This terrified them and they asked, 'What have you done?' (They knew he was running away from the Lord, because he had already told them so.) The sea was getting rougher and rougher. So they asked him, 'What should we do to you to make the sea calm down for us?'

'Pick me up and throw me into the sea,' he replied, 'and it will become calm. I know that it is my fault that this great storm has come upon you.' Instead the men did their best to row back to land. But they could not, for the sea grew even wilder than before. Then they cried to the Lord, 'O Lord, please do not let us die for taking this man's life. Do not hold us accountable for killing an innocent man, for you, O Lord, have done as you pleased.'" (1:7-14).

On Jonah's ship, the sailors' world was collapsing. Their gods had failed them. They had no place to turn except to God's man. Two problems! The Mediterranean was churning, and God's man was snoozing. How ironic that the one person on board who could have cried out to the real God wasn't available! Perhaps Jonah had taken some Sominex, but it was the exhaustion and depression caused by sin which really put God's man into a deep sleep.

If Jonah had been walking in fellowship with the Lord, he could have been the healing salt for the sailors instead of the cause of their troubles. Jesus said to His believers: *"You are the salt of the earth. But if the salt loses its saltiness, how can it be made salty again? It is no longer good for anything, except to be thrown out and trampled by men" (Matthew 5:13).* Instead of providing answers, Tarshish Christians create bigger problems. A man out of fellowship with God is a menace not only to himself, but to everyone he encounters.

God intends for believers to be the antidote to the corruptive forces of this world. He has no alternative plan. However, Christians in Tarshish exert no positive influence. They are "good for nothing" according to Jesus.

Consider Lot. The New Testament refers to him as a

"righteous man," one who was justified (II Peter 2:7-8). Lot was saved but sorry. He pictures everything a believer should not be. Lot held the destiny of Sodom and Gomorrah in his hands. He could have saved these cities if he had been able to influence just nine people in righteous ways.

God had promised Abraham that He would spare the evil cities if He could find ten righteous people in them (Genesis 18:32). If Lot had been able to reach just his own family members, the cities would have been saved. Lot compromised, however, and lost his testimony, his wife, his kids, and all that was dear to him—all for the opportunity to make a few bucks in those wicked, perverse cities. Lot chose to live in Sodom (spelled T-a-r-s-h-i-s-h), and his resulting lifestyle led to the destruction of many people.

Similarly, if the United States is ever destroyed, Tarshish-dwelling *believers* will have to shoulder the full responsibility for the downfall. We love to blame everyone—Republicans or Democrats, the economy, cults, Communists, humanists, spouses, or pastors! But God's promise to Israel applies to us in principle: *"If my people who are called by my name, will humble themselves and pray and seek my face and turn from their wicked ways, then will I hear from heaven and will forgive their sin and will heal their land" (II Chronicles 7:14).*

Revival will never begin in Tarshish. We can beg for it, pray for it, or cry for it, but any true spiritual awakening will start in the city square of downtown Nineveh. Christians are the salt of the earth only when their mail is addressed to Nineveh. Only from Nineveh do we calm storms rather than cause them. Tarshish-believers hurt everyone they touch—at home, at school, at work, at church, or at play.

Lesson 5:
Backsliders can look good and fool others.

Jonah was forced to go public when the sailors urged him to call on his god. These pagans had to drag out of him who he was and what he stood for. He drew on his spiritual heritage and offered a beautiful testimony: *"I am a Hebrew and I worship the Lord, the God of heaven, who made the sea and the land."* He was considerate of others: *"Pick me up and throw me into the sea, and it will become calm."* Some of the time he was truthful: *"I know that it is my fault that this great storm has come upon you."* In spite of these winsome traits, Jonah was stubborn about his sin. His walk did not match his talk. His testimony was a mockery. His request, *"Throw me into the sea,"* was a way of saying, "I would rather die than obey God." If Jonah had been rational, he would have said, "I repent of my sin. Please turn the boat around." The storm would then have subsided, and we would have no story of "Jonah and the Whale." Rebellious sinners are always misled in their thinking. Death by drowning seemed more profitable than life according to God.

Backsliders often know the right words and the right clichés to keep them in good standing with their fellow church members. Fooling pastors and church leaders is easy, at least for a while. A Sunday morning smile is easy to showcase. Jonah looked and sounded so good aboard ship that today we might be tempted to make him a deacon and give him a class of boys to teach.

Because backsliding always begins in the heart, the public cannot see a person's true spiritual condition. How difficult though to live as a fake, feigning a spiritual life, ever aware that the Lord knows the truth and that others will someday discover it!

**Lesson 6:
Gaining converts is not proof of
a person's spiritual condition.**

In the midst of Jonah's disobedience, the ship's crew came to know the Lord. *"Then they took Jonah and threw him overboard, and the raging sea grew calm. At this the men greatly feared the Lord, offered a sacrifice, and made vows to Him (1:15-16).*

Though Jonah failed these sailors in the hour of desperate need, they appear to have trusted his God. Some might refer to Jonah as a "soul-winner," but it certainly wasn't to his credit that these men were saved.

Jonah was consistent. He was willing to let both Nineveh and these heathen sailors die in ignorance of the true God. Fortunately, the Lord had used Jonah's weak, half-hearted testimony to bring about the salvation of these men. Later He would use the same anemic prophet to save the big city. The Word of God is powerful, even when it is delivered by a rebellious sinner.

In this day of cheap evangelism, there is a tendency to judge spirituality by "how many souls we've won." Jonah shows that reaching the lost does not depend primarily on the human vessel who is used. Converts do not even prove that the evangelist is in the will of God. Jonah cannot be held up as a model believer, but he could boast good "soul-winning" statistics—a whole boatload of sailors!

The heathen sailors were more honorable than Jonah. They showed more concern for one life than Jonah had for hundreds of thousands living in Nineveh. They tried hard to deliver their backslidden passenger. Valuable cargo was cast overboard, and the sailors rowed harder to save him. Only as a last resort did they throw Jonah into the deep.

**Lesson 7:
Just one wrong step makes a return difficult.**

Jonah had a "whale of a time" getting back to Nineveh. One rebellious move caused months, probably years, of torment.

One Night; One Lifetime

One wrong date, one drink, one crooked business deal, or even the purchase of one boat can cause years, even a lifetime, of spiritual bankruptcy. In a pastorate many years ago I watched two beautiful young Christian girls with missionary aspirations suffer spiritual shipwreck that ruined their lives. Just one prom (and the resulting misconduct), and things were never the same for either of them. And how many people would be alcoholics today if they had never taken that first social drink? We would do well to cultivate a great fear of sin.

Just one move out of the will of God can lead to a lifetime in Tarshish. Of course, the remedy is always available. The worst of sins can be confessed, and the worst of sinners can be restored. When we confess our self-serving, life-wrecking sin, then acknowledge Jesus as "Boss," we can enter the abundant life of Nineveh.

Lesson 8:
God always deals with backsliders.

"The Lord provided a great fish to swallow Jonah, and Jonah was inside the fish three days and three nights" (1:17).

God is like the Canadian mounted police: "He always gets His man." He sent a storm, then He awakened His sleeping prophet. When the sailors cast the dice, Jonah's number just happened to come up. What we call *"luck"* is really providence! *"The lot is cast into the lap, but its every decision is from God" (Proverbs 16:33).* When the sailors were forced to throw Jonah overboard, God said to His fish, "Jaws, swim next to that boat. When you see a splash, that's your lunch!" The Sovereign Lord wasn't going to twiddle His thumbs while Jonah sang "I Did It My Way!"

A Fish Story You Can Believe

Some preachers portray this fish as God's punishment for Jonah. Not so! This was God's fish of preservation, Jonah's life raft. The Lord was not yet finished with His wayward prophet. God was in control! Imagine the consequences if the fish had shown up five minutes late! We cannot overestimate God's sovereignty in finding the fish and sending it off on this particular errand of rescue.

After all, Jaws was not looking forward to this distasteful dinner, a backslider on his stomach for three days! (Have you ever lived in the same house with one?). Theologians argue about whether Jaws was a fish or a whale. Whichever he was, he had a whale of a constitution!

This creature was obedient. If the fish had emulated Jonah and said, "Not me, God," then took a deep dive into the Mediterranean, Nineveh might still be waiting for the Gospel. However, he did exactly what the Lord told him to do. All creation yields to the Sovereign Lord of the universe, with the exception of men and demons. Isn't it awesome that God does not give up on us? He still had Nineveh on His heart, but His revival plan would have to wait until He could rescue and restore His wandering child. Look what the Lord had to work with—an obedient fish and a disobedient preacher!

Jonah and the fish furnish a startling contrast. Better to be a dumb brute beast who obeys God than a smart, rational, cocky, egocentric member of the human race who disobeys Him!

Lesson 9:
The way to Nineveh is a Coronation Service.

When Jesus is acknowledged as King, we move into the Spirit-controlled life. The apostle Paul gave us clear instructions how to respond to the Gospel: *"Therefore I urge you, brothers, in view of God's mercy, to offer your bodies as living sacrifices, holy, and pleasing to God—which is your spiritual worship" (Romans 12:1).* Claiming Jesus as Lord involves a once-for-all presentation of our bodies on the altar of sacrifice, turning all rights over to Him. When this is accomplished, God moves us into downtown Nineveh.

How far is Nineveh from Tarshish? On the map, it is

about 2000 miles. In our spiritual pilgrimage, it is only a Coronation Service away. It's that glorious time of surrender when we confess our own unworthiness, then "bring forth the royal diadem and crown Him Lord of all." This is not a time to fear what we are going to lose, or what we are going to have to "give up." When Peter said to Jesus, *"We have left everything to follow you,"* Jesus replied, *"No one who has left home or brothers or sisters or mother or father or children or fields for me and the gospel will fail to receive a hundred times as much in this present age (homes, brothers, sisters, mothers, children and fields—and with them, persecutions) and in the age to come, eternal life" (Mark 10:28-30).* The King promises to take great care of His subjects!

What an amazing God! He created Jonah, then kept him alive for three days and three nights inside a fish that He had also created. However, the miracle of the fish pales in comparison to the greater miracle, His love for His runaway child.

CHAPTER TWO

RUNNING TO GOD

Skeptics argue about whether a man could be swallowed by a fish and live to tell about it. The problem is solved in rather simple fashion when by faith we acknowledge that our sovereign God created both the fish and the man. Directing the fish to swallow the man or keeping the man alive for three days and three nights would be no problem for the Creator of the world. These are mere trivialities for the Sovereign Lord of the universe.

After All, Jonah Was Only a Minor Prophet!

Well-documented cases speak of whales swallowing horses and fish swallowing men, with the victims surviving the ordeals. An exhibit in Chicago's Field Museum tells of a man living through such an experience and suffering only minor consequences, such as baldness and wrinkled skin. (Have you noticed any resurrected backsliders in your congregation?).

In 1881, a man named James Bartley fell overboard and was swallowed by a whale. Two days later the whale was killed, and the man was found alive. After several weeks Bartley recovered from the shock and resumed a normal life. His only problem was that the fish's digestive juices burned his skin, and he was bleached to a deadly whiteness.

Many other reports give evidence of people being swallowed by fish and living to tell about it. However, the truth about Jonah does not rest on how many human experiences we can relate. If God had so desired, He could have used a sardine with bad teeth! Believers should be able to accept Jonah's experience without reservation because the Bible is God's Truth. God cannot lie, and He certainly has no desire to deceive us.

A friend recently shared this refreshing story of a young believer on an airplane flight. A man seated next to her was ridiculing her faith and got around to the age-old question, "Could the whale have swallowed Jonah?"

"I don't know," the young lady replied. "I'll have to ask Jonah when I get to Heaven."

"But what if Jonah's not in Heaven?" the skeptic asked.

"Then you'll have to ask him!"

The conversation abruptly ended!

A. Now that I'm Here, I don't Like it

"From inside the fish Jonah prayed to the Lord his God. He said: 'In my distress I called to the Lord, and he answered me. From the depths of the grave ['belly of hell'— KJV] I called for help, and you listened to my cry' " (2:1-2).

What is it like for a believer to be out of fellowship with the Lord? Here we get a glimpse of the backslider's hell. The "belly of hell" (sheol) refers to the grave or the place of the departed. Jonah had run from God; now he's terrified about being away. Fortunately, even the inner parts of a Mediterranean fish cannot clog the channels of prayer.

Jonah did not refer to the eternal hell which awaits anyone who rejects Christ. He does seem, however, to set up a comparison between the backslider's awful situation on earth and the place of eternal punishment. A backslider's life is certainly no Sunday School picnic! Jonah experienced untold misery and terror while he was in Fish College!

A Sleazy Underwater Hotel

Splashing in the icy cold water shocked Jonah, as God confronted him with physical, mental, and spiritual disturbances.

Jonah described his physical torment

"You hurled me into the deep, into the very heart of the seas, and the currents swirled about me; all your waves and

breakers swept over me. I said, 'I have been banished from your sight; yet I will look again toward your holy temple.' The engulfing waters threatened me, the deep surrounded me, seaweed was wrapped around my head. To the roots of the mountains I sank down; the earth beneath barred me in forever. But you brought my life up from the pit, O Lord my God." (2:3-6).

A backslider often suffers many needless physical ailments. Jonah described the agony of being helpless against the currents swirling around him and the waves crushing upon him. God's disobedient servant was engulfed in seaweed, gastric juices were taking their toll on his hair and skin, waters were continually passing over him, and there was no air conditioning. What displeasure!

A report in Chicago's Field Museum states that, when a fish inhales, his stomach is 90% full of water and when he exhales, he is only 60% full. (Jonah, how do you spell "relief?" E-x-h-a-l-e!!!)

When sin characterizes our lives, we often experience similar physical discomfort. A careless carnal Christian with unconfessed sin can empathize with Jonah. It is possible to sit comfortably in church and hurt in the belly of a fish at the same time. Certainly not all illnesses and injuries result from the Tarshish-life, but many do. The guilt, fear, and worry associated with sinful living cause many ailments that only a trip to Nineveh can cure.

Christians suffer needlessly when living away from the Lord. Surely God did not save us to be bouncing around in a fish's belly with a 10% to 40% breathing capacity. Spirit-filled believers in downtown Nineveh can expect to be generally healthier than carnal believers elsewhere. The stress of Tarshish-living often increases doctor and hospital bills.

Jonah told of his spiritual troubles

When Jonah complained, *"I have been banished from your sight,"* he felt cut off from God. Of course, God was still very much alive and alert, not banished from a single part of Jonah's experiences. From the prophet's perspective, however, God was dead, or maybe on vacation. The Lord never seems to be present when we are faking our spiritual condition. It's worth the price of a trip to Nineveh just to make our loving God seem real again.

Jonah complained of mental problems

How terrorizing to be at the bottom of the sea! The mind of a rebel Christian becomes saturated with thoughts of Nineveh and what life could have been. Some look to sports to bring relief from self-centered lives, but the Nineveh Yankees always beat the Tarshish Braves in the World Series! And the Nineveh Steelers beat the Tarshish Cowboys in the Super Bowl! Others try to find a release with music, but the concert furnishes little joy when the orchestra features "The Nineveh Polka" or "Way Down upon the Tigris River."

Jonah spoke of sinking to the roots of the mountains, where the earth beneath barred him in forever. However, in that horrendous situation, Jonah reached that beautiful spot which the Psalmist referred to as *"wits' end" (Psalm 107:27)*. In his prayer Jonah quoted from several Psalms so he may have been familiar with the description of this other storm at sea. The Lord stirred up a tempest which caused some merchant seamen to reach their wits' end. *"Others went out on the sea in ships; they were merchants on the mighty waters. They saw the works of the Lord, his wonderful deeds in the deep. For he spoke and stirred up a tempest that lifted high the waves. They mounted up to the heavens and went down to the depths; in their peril their courage melted away. They reeled and staggered like drunken men; they were at their wits' end. Then they cried out to the Lord in their trouble, and he brought them out of their distress. He stilled the storm to a whisper; the waves of the sea were hushed. They were glad when it grew calm, and he guided them to their desired haven. Let them give thanks to the Lord for his unfailing love and his wonderful deeds for men" (Psalm 107:23-31)*. These sailors showed great wisdom in dealing with their problem and were led out of their distress. Jonah had failed a similar stress test aboard the ship, but now at his wits' end in the fish's belly he has been brought to a turning point in his life.

Wits' End may be a tough place, but it can become a truly meaningful experience. If we respond properly when we reach wits' end, we realize how frail and inadequate we are. We cannot live the Christian life in our own strength and cannot cope with life's problems apart from our Lord. Many psychiatrists and counselors would lose a lot of fees if believers moved from Wits' End to downtown Nineveh.

B. Theology Lessons from Fish Seminary

The Psalmist said: *"Before I was afflicted, I went astray, but now I obey your word." (Psalm 119:87).* For Jonah, the fish-ride brought about a significant change, the kind that could show us how we might avoid a similar experience, Jonah had not prayed when he was at the Joppa Travel Agency or on the ship, but now aboard the fish he spent three days and nights in "submarine praying." Sometimes God has to use extreme measures to get our attention.

Lesson 1:
Affliction Teaches Us to Pray

Jonah's prayer was remarkable. In spite of his life-threatening dilemma, he did not utter one single petition for himself. He did not even ask God for deliverance from the fish. Instead of making requests, he merely reviewed God's promised blessings from several psalms and claimed them as his own. Praying from the Scriptures may well be the highest form of prayer.

God has so much more to offer than does this world. This was not the time for Jonah to hear man's philosophy, best summed up with "grin and bear it, and keep a stiff upper lip." And man's ever-changing psychology might urge Jonah to "look on the good side." (In a fish's belly?) This was not the time for churchianity, either consolation through church rituals such as baptism or from liberal theology. (It's difficult to "do good and live clean" amid seaweed and gastric juices.) "Possibility thinking" does not seem right for such a time as this. As for the charismatic approach, "Just don't receive the whale,"—well, it's pretty hard to deny a whale! Such humanistic religious endeavors prove to be totally ineffective in the belly of a fish.

Fortunately the weakened, run-down prophet realized that "salvation comes from the Lord." True deliverance led him to God's infallible source, the Word! Praying Jonah-style, out of God's Word, is highly effective worship and does bring deliverance.

Lesson 2:
Whatever Goes Down Must Come Up—Spiritual Gravity

"When my life was ebbing away, I remembered you, Lord, and my prayer rose to you, to your holy temple. Those who cling to worthless idols forfeit the grace that could be theirs. But I, with a song of thanksgiving, will sacrifice to you. What I have vowed, I will make good. Salvation comes from the Lord" (2:7-9).

God uses our inner dissatisfaction and craving for spiritual reality to drive us to the same conclusion which Jonah confessed. Here is the key that unlocks the city-gate to Nineveh: *"When my life was ebbing away, I remembered you, Lord"(2:7).* From Wits' End, Jonah confessed his lying vanities—thinking that he could run from God, then run his own life. He acknowledged clinging to worthless idols that deprived him of God's matchless grace and almost cost him his life. Idols always prove themselves untrustworthy and impotent. It is important to notice that Jonah's idols were not carved objects. His major idol was himself—empty vanity! He had not been able to get God's perspective because he was totally immersed in his own selfish conceit. Now the humbled prophet has given evidence of a heart resigned to the sovereign will of God. He recognized his only true hope: *"Salvation comes from the Lord" (2:9).*

Lesson 3:
The Three R's

The tuition cost was unbelievably high, but Jonah gained some valuable insights inside the fish's belly. From God's curriculum he learned the three R's that bring a calm peace to rebellious sinners: Rebuke, Restoration, and Return. God never discards a child of His. The repentant runaway was once again qualified for service.

Lesson 4:
You Can't Keep a Good Man Down

"And the Lord commanded the fish, and it vomited Jonah onto dry land" (2:10).

As He does in every life, God spoke the last word in Jonah's experience. Jonah learned that he could not thwart God's eternal purpose.

Lesson 5:
The Place of Departure Is The Place of Return

When Jonah finally admitted that salvation was of the

Lord, God beached the fish, and the fish beached Jonah. How glad that poor fish was to obey! Three days and three nights spent with a backslider should be reported to the Society for the Prevention of Cruelty to Animals. That fish, minus his nauseating cargo, was undoubtedly the happiest creature in the sea.

At what geographic location did the fish beach Jonah? I am quite sure that the answer is *Joppa*, right back where he had started running on his route of rebellion. We get back in where we got out, with lots of time wasted. It takes only an instant to get right with God, but we can never reclaim those lost opportunities.

Lesson 6:
If at First You Don't Succeed

Chapter three introduces us to the God of second chances and new beginnings. A comparison of Chapter 3:1-2 with Chapter 1:1-2 shows that Jonah could have saved himself a lot of time (and shortened this book) if he had simply obeyed God the first time. Through Jonah's lengthy rebellion, God's commission remained unchanged: *"The word of the Lord came to Jonah a second time, 'Go to the great city of Nineveh and proclaim to it the message I give you'"* (3:1-2). The next verse begins with the submissive word *"so" (3:3)* instead of the rebellious *"but" (1:3)*. *"So Jonah obeyed the word of the Lord and went to Nineveh"* (3:3). In chapter one he arose and fled; in chapter three he arose and went. Jonah decided to do it God's way. The do-it-my-own-way approach had failed him utterly.

God does not change His mind about what He calls us to do. *"God's gifts and His call are irrevocable" (Romans 11:29).* Our stubborn rebellion may in some cases make it difficult, even impossible, to later be obedient, but God's call is never withdrawn. A calling to a specific ministry long ago, whether obeyed or not, is still valid today.

If I were God, the Book of Jonah would have contained only three verses. Jonah would have been been blown to bits when he set sail for Tarshish. However, our patient Lord loves us dearly and does not give up on us quickly. It may take a fish-ride to teach us obedience, but God never quits wooing His children to live in His will. We learn, often too late, that His way is always best for us and for the ones we are to serve.

A simple Coronation Service moves a self-serving believer back into the center of God's will. This requires an acknowledgment that Jesus Christ bore our sins in His own body on Calvary's tree: *"God made him who had no sin to be sin for us, so that in him we might become the righteousness of God" (II Corinthians 5:21).* Our sins were imputed to Jesus' account. The Heavenly Father punished Him in our behalf. During the three hours of darkness while He hung on the Cross, Jesus suffered everything that the Bible tells us about Hell. This makes Calvary a very personal issue for each of us. It was *our* sin that caused His suffering and death. Upon receiving Him as Lord and Savior, we rejoice in the fact that God also imputed Christ's righteousness to our account. What a swap when we are saved by grace, our sin for God's Son!

In response to this matchless Calvary love, the sinner is

instructed: *"That if you confess with your mouth, 'Jesus is Lord' and believe in your heart that God raised him from the dead, you will be saved. For it is with your heart that you believe and are justified, and it is with your mouth that you confess and are saved" (Romans 10:9-10).* Jesus paid the Hell-price for our sin so that He could become the Lord of every believer. *"For this very reason, Christ died and returned to life so that he might be the Lord of both the dead and the living" (Romans 14:9).*

Jesus becomes personal Lord when we respond properly to Calvary: *"Therefore, I urge you, brothers, in view of God's mercy, to offer your bodies as living sacrifices, holy and pleasing to God—this is your spiritual act of worship" (Romans 12:1).* We are required to present our bodies to the Lord in a once-for-all act of total commitment, relinquishing full ownership rights to Him. Acknowledgment of Jesus as Boss moves a believer right out of the despair of Tarshish into the fullness of the Nineveh life. Obedience is the key: *"Trust in the Lord with all your heart* [Nineveh], *and lean not on your own understanding* [Tarshish]; *in all your ways acknowledge him, and he will make your paths straight" (Proverbs 3:5-6).*

A few years ago, an influential deacon in a California church departed from a service sobbing convulsively. As I talked with him, he confessed that he had been living in Tarshish for almost thirty years. After examining the reality of his salvation, I shared with him that he was just a Coronation Service away from Nineveh. I told him that he needed to yield his body to the Lord on the altar of sacrifice, thus receiving Jesus as his Sovereign Boss. Although he left in pathetic condition, he returned the next evening overflowing with joy. He reported to the church that he had settled the Lordship issue on his bed the previous night. He testified that, although he was a charter member and a hardworking pillar of the church, his fellow members had never had the opportunity to see him right with God. He asked them to forgive him for the useless church work he had done in the flesh for the past thirty years. Needless to say, a genuine revival spirit broke out that evening.

Life becomes abundant ("more than enough") when Jesus is Lord (Boss!).

CHAPTER THREE

RUNNING WITH GOD

"*Then the word of the Lord came to Jonah a second time: 'Go to the great city of Nineveh and proclaim to it the message I give you.'* " *(3:1-2).* After running *from* God (chapter one) Jonah ran back *to* Him (chapter two). In chapter three Jonah was finally running *with* God, resulting in what is perhaps the greatest revival in human history.

A Preacher Smelling Like Sardines?

Very likely Jonah was a tragic spectacle as he journeyed into Nineveh. No revival posters or billboards to advertise the meetings! Smelling strongly of fish, bald, scratching his scaly skin, Jonah certainly lacked the flamboyant look of a typical evangelist. The local ministerial group simply wasn't too impressed. Fortunately the true message hides the messenger.

A Mouthful of Saltwater Makes a Lasting Impression

God has a sense of humor. The national god of Assyria was Dagon, the *fish-god*. All around the city were replicas of this false god with his fish-body and a human head. Also, one of Nineveh's most popular goddesses had the body of a woman and the head of a fish. (I may have seen her at the mall last week!). Everywhere the poor evangelist turned, he was reminded of the three days and nights he spent in the aquarium!

The highlight of this chapter is the description of the greatest revival in history. A spirit of repentance gripped the hearts of the people so that God's intended judgment was averted. All the way from the king to the lowest subjects there was a genuine turning away from evil. True revival had come to the hated enemies of Israel. Some scholars believe that every person in Nineveh turned to Jehovah. The revival was long-lasting. National repentance delayed God's destruction of the city for about 150 years. However, the people evidently fell back into deep sin, so the prophet Nahum later told of the final destruction of Nineveh.

Today we stand in the most crucial hours of American history. God is speaking to us just as he did to Nineveh. Judgment is facing us unless we repent. Our greatest need is for a God-sent nationwide revival reaching from the top to the bottom of our social order.

A. Why Did Revival Come to Nineveh?

1. The Obedient Prophet

"Jonah obeyed the word of the Lord and went to Nineveh. Now Nineveh was a very important city—a visit required three days" (3:3).

Although Jonah bore no resemblance to a professional clergyman, he did bear the marks of resurrection. He was now an obedient servant, the basic requirement for being used by God. As was later revealed, this was sullen obedience. We have no reason to believe that Jonah had changed his prejudices about the Assyrians. Apparently he had suffered so much through his disobedient days that he had no other option but to preach. In spite of his attitude, the amazing sovereignty of God brought the people of Nineveh to repentance. Jonah may not have been right, but his message was straight, so God honored His Word.

A Sign to Nineveh?

Jesus preached, *"For as Jonah was a sign to the Ninevites, so also will the Son of Man be to this generation"* (Luke 11:30). But how could Jonah be a sign from God?

Dr. Alan Redpath, former pastor of the Moody Church in Chicago, suggests an interesting thought: "Jonah is flung into the sea; up jumps a big fish, and down Jonah goes, and the sailors see it happen. In a moment the sea becomes calm. Then they take stock and they worship God, and they say,

'Now what shall we do? We were going to Tarshish; no use going there now, we lost the cargo, we flung it overboard. The only thing is to go back to Joppa, get another cargo, and get the ship repaired; we're in bad shape and will never make it.' So they went back to Joppa. If that happened, I am quite sure the news of Jonah's deliverance had reached Nineveh before he got there. When he arrived he was a sign to the people. He was a man alive from the dead."

Jonah had the mark of death upon him, yet he was alive again—a resurrected man, a sign! Revival came in Nineveh, not because Jonah could do miracles, but because he *was* a miracle!

2. Truth from Heaven—a Message from God

"On the first day, Jonah started into the city. He proclaimed: 'Forty more days and Nineveh will be overturned' " (3:4).

Jonah faithfully proclaimed the message God gave him. Just eight words, certainly not a popular crowd-pleasing sermon! The Spirit of God used it, however, to drive the king and his subjects to repentance in sackcloth and ashes.

Someone has suggested that if Jonah were ministering today, he would use his experiences to lecture on "The Existential Value of Seaweed" or "The Nutritional Value of Whale-blubber." Perhaps revival is waiting for preachers who will proclaim the message God gives, no matter how unpopular or offensive it might be. Not great theological or philosophical discourses, just the truth about the Sovereign God who has redeemed this world from sin.

Today many churches are facing a dilemma. The craze for big numbers has kept some pastors from preaching against sin or demanding repentance. The common explanation is that such preaching offends people and drives them away. Jonah's revival-inspiring sermon would not fit the agenda of most churches today. Repentance is as unpopular now as when poor Jonah had to preach it. The current "user-friendly" messages, however, are not consistent with the nature of the Cross.

The Cross has always been an offense to sinners, but it is *"the power of God for the salvation of everyone who believes" (Romans 1:16)*. The Gospel [Jesus' death, burial and resurrection] is also the power behind successful Christian living: *"to us who are being saved it* [the Cross] *is the power of God" (I Corinthians 1:18)*. Recently, I have attended services in which the Cross (that is, the Gospel) was not referred to in either song or sermon, even though such topics as forgiveness and overcoming temptation were being taught. What should deeply concern us is the good response to such services. People even "get saved" without the Gospel, which is both scary and impossible. Absence of Gospel preaching may well be our nation's most significant problem. Big attendance and good statistics may result, but such "worship" certainly hinders the kind of Nineveh revival we so desperately need.

Paul stated the issue plainly: *"For since in the wisdom of God the world through its wisdom did not know him, God was pleased through the foolishness of what was preached to save those who believe. Jews demand miraculous signs and Greeks look for wisdom, but we preach Christ crucified: a stumbling block to Jews and foolishness to Gentiles, but to those whom God has called, both Jews and Greeks, Christ the power of God and the wisdom of God. For the foolishness of God is wiser than man's wisdom, and the weakness of God is stronger than man's strength" (I Corinthians 1:21-25)*. He added: *"For I resolved to know nothing while I was with you except Jesus Christ and him crucified" (I Corinthians 2:2)*. Just as Jonah did not resort to a "user friendly" message in Nineveh, such sermons played no part in Paul's world-changing ministry, and they should have no place in our services today.

Highlights of Jonah's Message

Jonah didn't bother much with homiletics or a classy three-point outline in which all the points started with the same letter! Neither did he strive to be popular with his hearers by sugar-coating his stern message. He simply passed on to the people what God had given him.

(1) A Note of Warning—
"Forty Days of Grace, Then Judgment"

God threatened to destroy the city in just forty days. Throughout the Scriptures, the number *"forty"* seems to be associated with God's testings. It is a time of waiting for divine activity: a forty day flood, Moses' forty years on the back side of the desert, Israel's forty years in the wilderness, and the Lord's forty days of temptation. Now, through His prophet, God plainly announced Nineveh's forty-day trial and His intention to destroy the sinful city. As always, however, the loving Lord extended a grace period before the coming judgment.

(2) A Sense of Urgency

Nineveh had to act immediately. God never leads His people to make decisions tomorrow: *"Do not boast about tomorrow, for you do not know what a day may bring forth" (Proverbs 27:1).*

Jesus tells us of the rich farmer who finally achieved success. He had everything he wanted, full barns and plenty of money, but his world came crashing down when he heard the Lord's voice: *"You fool! This very night your life will be demanded from you. Then who will get what you have prepared for yourself? This is how it will be with anyone who stores up things for himself but is not rich toward God" (Luke 12:20-21).* Every obituary and every grave preaches an urgent challenge that should lead us to instant obedience. God does not settle for less.

When God calls His people to any spiritual endeavor, He demands immediate response, not after family issues are solved, or financial problems are worked out, or after we "pray about it." Even if circumstances prevent the immediate carrying out of His assignment, He wants instant submission to it.

"One More Night with the Frogs"

Billy Sunday, the old-time major league baseball player turned evangelist (poor guy never got to play for the Yankees), preached a sermon exposing the folly of spiritual procrastination. This masterpiece centers around an unbelievable verse, Exodus 8:10.

As Egypt was suffering from the latest of God's plagues, frogs covered the land. Frogs everywhere—in the bedroom, kitchen, parlor, even in the oven! We can imagine many strange scenes: Egyptians screaming at their strange bedfellows, girls finding frogs in their curlers, women baking angel-frog cakes, boys squishing frogs on the way to school, even the game being called because of frogs. No way of escape! Croaking, deafening sounds! Repulsive to the touch! Hard on the nose, dead frogs piled in heaps! Egypt *had* to get rid of those frogs!

Pharaoh finally asked Moses to intercede with God: "*Moses said to Pharaoh, 'I leave to you the honor of setting the time for me to pray for you and your officials and your people that you and your houses may be rid of the frogs, except for those that remain in the Nile.'* " We would expect Pharaoh to shout frantically, "The sooner the better," but instead he replied, *"Tomorrow" (Exodus 8:10).* Think of it! Pharaoh actually requested one more night in the miserable company of the frogs!

Pharaoh Is Not Alone in His Folly

This request for a delay would be totally unbelievable were it not for the multitudes of people who practice the same logic in spiritual matters. How often a proud, rebellious person, plagued with the misery and despair of sin, shows an interest in God's gracious offer of salvation but requests one more night in the clutches of sin. The marvelous life of Christ is put off for "one more night," which often stretches into a lifetime, followed by an endless eternity.

Or how often does the Lord stand by a Christian plagued by the troubles, doubts, and heartaches of Tarshish-living, only to hear the desperate self-server say, "Not now. Give me a little while longer to run my own life in my own miserable way. Give me one more night with the frogs before I move into Your glory?"

This same attitude of procrastination often grips entire churches who need to repent and rekindle revival fires. Most knowledgeable Christians have good intentions about "someday." Meanwhile, we choose to continue with the frogs of fear, frustration, fighting, and futility, simply because our pride doesn't allow us to admit our sinfulness. We opt for more time of compromise and misery.

God does have deadlines. Jonah's message to the Ninevites did not allow for any delay. His warning of destruction called for *immediate* repentance. God was about to act. The end was near. His time for repentance was "right now," the same timetable He uses in all His dealings with man. The results of procrastination can be horror-filled: *"A man who remains stiff-necked after many rebukes will suddenly be destroyed without remedy" (Proverbs 29:1).*

"Lord, This Can't Wait"

Bud was an alcoholic master-sergeant who became a regular attender at all of our worship services in Taiwan. Although he recognized his lost condition and showed considerable interest in the Gospel, he remained unconverted because of his deep loyalty to a traditional church. His association with Christians, however, did bring an end to his drinking problems.

One Sunday afternoon Bud met five of his ex-drinking buddies in the Sergeant's Club. All were suffering hangovers and headaches from their weekend partying. When one friend expressed a desire for a better way of life, Bud began to tell him about the exciting life available in Christ.

Having heard so many times about Christ's redeeming work at Calvary, Bud found it easy to share salvation, until it dawned on him that he himself was a lost man. Excusing himself for a moment, he turned around in his chair and quietly said, "Lord, save me *quick*," then turned immediately to share his new-found faith with his friend. That night Bud testified to all of us how he had been born again that afternoon. He returned to the Air Base in a wet uniform, having been baptized to picture his faith. In just a few seconds, God gave Bud eternal life. In just a few seconds, Bud shared with his friends about his new Lord. Within a few hours, Bud obediently and publicly pictured his union with the Lord in death, burial, and resurrection. What a day!

This sense of urgency that caused Bud to turn so quickly to the Lord should grip all of us. No lost person is promised a tomorrow in which to get saved, and no believer has a promise of added time for yielding to God's will. *Today* is always the time for spiritual action and obedience.

(3) A Life-Changing Truth: "Salvation Comes from the Lord"

The heart of Jonah's message grew out of his experience in the fish: *"Salvation comes from the Lord" (2:9).* Jonah was aware that the gods of Assyria could do nothing for these pagan people. Salvation could come only from his God, *"the Lord, the God of heaven, who made the sea and the land" (1:9).* He could not compromise by preaching polite lies, such as "one god is as good as another" or "we're all going the same place, just taking different roads." Jonah knew that these Ninevites had to look ahead through the centuries to the Messiah's approaching blood atonement for their redemption.

3. The Response of the People

"The Ninevites believed God. They declared a fast, and all of them, from the greatest to the least, put on sackcloth. When the news reached the king of Nineveh, he rose from his throne, took off his royal robes, covered himself with sackcloth and sat down in the dust. Then he issued a proclamation in Nineveh: 'By the decree of the king and his nobles: Do not

let any man or beast, herd or flock, taste anything; do not let them eat or drink. But let man and beast be covered with sackcloth. Let everyone call urgently on God. Let them give up their evil ways and their violence. Who knows? God may yet relent and with compassion turn from his fierce anger so that we will not perish.' When God saw what they did and how they turned from their evil ways, he had compassion and did not bring upon them the destruction he had threatened" (3:5-10).

Certainly God had not condoned the wickedness, the crimes, or the inhumanity of the citizens of Nineveh. On the contrary, these undesirable pagans were convicted in their hearts and turned from their evil ways. Even more certainly, Jonah's journey to Nineveh didn't mean that he loved or pitied these sinful foreigners. He was simply obeying the Lord, but with great reluctance.

In our time we also are called to take the life-giving Gospel to societies that may engage in practices we consider repugnant. The fact that we don't approve of certain lifestyles doesn't excuse us from our responsibility. Jonah was obedient to the heavenly call, and his obedience saved and changed an entire city. The people heard God speaking through him.

How Did This Funny-Looking Evangelist Persuade the People?

What was it about Jonah that caused the king and hundreds of thousands of people to repent? First, some major catastrophes in nature may have struck fear in their hearts. They thought their city was an impregnable fortress.

It was protected by both an outer wall and an inner one. The inner wall was fifty feet wide, one hundred feet high, and about eight miles in circumference. The outer wall encompassed fields and small towns. Nothing seemingly could destroy them. However, just a few years before Jonah arrived, two foreboding plagues of famine had devastated the region, and a few months before his visit, a total eclipse of the sun had scared them. These events were considered to be signs of divine anger, so their hearts were perhaps softened a bit toward hearing God's messenger.

The second thing that may have caused the people to obey God was this strange-looking man who had come to preach to them. His encounter with the fish certainly would have affected his appearance. We previously mentioned about a sailor who fell overboard and was swallowed by a large whale. Rescued two days later, the man recovered, but the whale's digestive juices had burned off his first layer of skin so that every feature of the man was white. That same thing may have happened to Jonah.

Imagine this albino man, a hated Jew, coming to this great Assyrian city and hearing people ask, "How come you are so white? You look strange." Jonah would answer, "Funny you should mention this. In forty days God is going to wipe out your city unless you repent. To prove that He can do it, let me share my story with you. I was on a ship trying to run away from this God, and He sent a great storm. When the sailors found out that I had caused the storm, they threw me into the sea. Just as I went under, this great fish came and swallowed me. While I was in the belly of the fish, I repented of my sin. I am here today to tell you that this same

God is going to destroy you unless you repent of your wicked ways."

If I were a Ninevite, I'd be tempted to say, "Hey, I believe!" This is why Jesus said that Jonah was a sign to the people of Nineveh, just as He Himself is to people everywhere.

Of course, the famines, the eclipse, and the odd-looking evangelist were not the major reasons why revival came to Nineveh. Such spiritual victory is always the supernatural work of the Holy Spirit in convicting people of their sin and showing them the righteousness that is in Christ Jesus. When we New Testament believers meet Jonah and the converted Ninevites in heaven, we will realize that all of us were saved in the same manner. Both Old Testament and New Testament believers have appropriated God's grace through obedient trust in the finished work—the death, burial, and resurrection—of the Messiah, our Lord Jesus. Saints of old looked ahead by faith to the Gospel that we look back upon.

Why Is That Hungry Cat in a Burlap Bag?

The pagan Assyrians accepted the Sovereign Lord's will for them and their city. They repented and turned from their evil ways. Even the king rose from his throne of authority and humiliated himself by putting on sackcloth (a scratchy burlap that symbolized his grief over sin). He then sat in ashes to show that he was contrite and believed the prophet's message. His remorse led him to issue a proclamation calling for repentance, prayer, and a radical lifestyle change. This edict required that even animals were to be draped in sackcloth and forced to fast, along with their owners, symbolically involving the whole population in remorse over sin and violence.

Revival broke out instantaneously as God responded with compassion: *"When God saw what they did and how they turned from their evil ways, he had compassion and did not bring upon them the destruction he had threatened" (3:10).* God is always committed to judging evil, but He is also committed to forgiving anyone who repents. Some find it difficult to believe that God changed His mind, but He had already pledged to do so whenever nations repent. *"If at any time I announce that a nation or kingdom is to be uprooted, torn down, and destroyed, and if that nation I warned repents of its evil, then I will relent and not inflict on it the disaster I had planned" (Jeremiah 18:7-8).* This promise might constitute America's greatest hope today.

Of course, when we talk about God changing His mind, we are talking from a human perspective. In reality, He doesn't change His mind. The all-knowing God knew in advance exactly what was going to happen in Nineveh. The revival came as no surprise to Him. He did not have to adjust His plans and purpose to accomodate it.

"Lord, Do It Again"

Learning about such a stirring revival should make us thirst for a similar outpouring of God's Spirit. Our nation stands in desperate need of spiritual awakening, the kind we have not experienced since Civil War days. Only in downtown Nineveh can we receive God's stirring revival power. Christians in Tarshish are barriers to blessing and hindrances to revival.

B. What Did Revival Bring to Nineveh?

What are the practical results of real revival? How do we know when we are living in downtown Nineveh? What is it like to be controlled by the Holy Spirit?

1. He Overcomes Hardship for Us: It's Not An Easy Road

The Spirit-filled life is not always blissful. The "prosperity cult" TV preachers, in order to satisfy the itching ears of selfish listeners, have spoken total untruth about the Spirit-filled life. Bubbly ecstasy with the accompanying smile and repeating of well-worn Christian clichés do not give an honest picture of a genuinely revived Christian. How sad to watch so-called "Spirit-filled" believers suggest that everything is always peaches and cream! Nineveh-life is not merely playing religious games. Total commitment can be tough. *Jesus said, "In the world you will have trouble. But take heart! I have overcome the world" (John 16:33).* When Paul, for example, was living spiritually in downtown Nineveh, he got jailed, stoned, ridiculed, and continually harassed. Jeremiah preached and served faithfully for about forty-six years, apparently without any converts, or even any encouragement. Nineveh-living is not easy living, but it is exciting and eternally rewarding.

2. He Fights for Us: "The Battle Is The Lord's"

Why should we expect a picnic in a world that has always hated the Christ who dwells within us? Why should we expect riches when He walked in poverty? The Bible never promises that faithful Christians will be rich, healthy, or free from trouble. The truth is, Christians are not even promised houses. Throughout the world today, many believers are homeless and persecuted. Spiritual prosperity is promised, but not material riches. Nothing in the Scriptures indicates that Christians will be either physically healthy or materially wealthy this side of eternity.

The Lord Jesus stated emphatically that this world would hate His disciples: *"If the world hates you, keep in mind that it hated me first. If you belonged to the world, it would love you as its own. As it is, you do not belong to the world, but I have chosen you out of the world. That is why the world hates you"* (John 15:18-19).

The comforting news is that we aren't responsible for fighting our own battles. Our warfare is with unseen forces, so Christians never *win* victories; we *receive* them from our Lord: *"Thanks be to God! He gives us the victory through our Lord Jesus Christ"* (I Corinthians 15:57). Over and over the Bible states that *"the battle is the Lord's!"* It was true for Israel, and it's just as true for us. When the Israelites were leaving Egypt, terrorized because Pharaoh and his army were in hot pursuit, Moses said: *"Stand firm and you will see the deliverance the Lord will bring you today. The Egyptians you see today you will never see again. The Lord will fight for you; you need only to be still" (Exodus 14:13-14).* Quite a difference from the competitive ratrace in Tarshish where we take matters into our own hands.

3. He Lives for Us: "Not I... But Christ Lives in Me"

The most thrilling aspect of life in Nineveh is *"Christ in you, the hope of glory."* While the world may not be enthused about dedicated Christians, a holy excitement should characterize those who live under the authority of the Lord Jesus. Our greatest privilege is to serve as God's dwelling place on earth: *"Do you not know that your body is a temple of the Holy Spirit, who is in you, whom you have received from God? You are not your own; you were bought at a price. Therefore honor God with your body" (I Corinthians 6:19-20).*

Peter challenged us to give the Lord His rightful place so that lost and erring friends would ask us to explain our victorious lifestyle: *"But in your hearts set apart Christ as Lord. Always be prepared to give an answer to everyone who asks you to give the reason for the hope that you have" (I Peter 3:15).* The people of this world have every right to see Christ living in us—changing us, purifying us, forgiving us, blessing our families, and assuring us of eternal life. However, others will see these life-transforming results only when our permanent address is downtown Nineveh. In Tarshish, we are not much different from the lost world. In fact, non-Christian friends often display more radiant lifestyles than self-serving believers.

4. He Thinks for Us: "We Have the Mind of Christ"

Above all, Christians who surrender to the Lord will learn what God is thinking, right from the written Word. The Apostle claimed a great treasure for believers: *"We have the mind of Christ" (I Corinthians 2:16).* Through Bible study, we come to know His will, and find it to be *"good, pleasing and perfect." (Romans 12:2).* In Nineveh we have no gripes or arguments with God. The harmful earthly philosophies which we have believed and practiced all our lives begin to be replaced with what the all-knowing God thinks and says! We no longer lean to our own understanding. We acknowledge Jesus as Lord, and He directs our paths. We discover that His thinking and His ways really are higher than ours: *"For my thoughts are not your thoughts, neither are your ways my ways, declares the Lord. As the heavens are higher than the earth, so are my ways higher than your ways and my thoughts than your thoughts" (Isaiah 55:8-9).*

What awesome revival would come to our lives, our homes, our churches, and our nation, if we submitted to God's thinking, recorded for us in an infallible Book. Learning the practical truths of God's Word is the greatest need in our nation today, so Bible study should be the prime activity of every church. The best of man's thinking will never bring the spiritual revival we so desperately need.

CHAPTER FOUR

RUNNING AHEAD OF GOD

T he Book of Jonah contains more miracles for its size than any other book. In chapter one, while Jonah was running away, the Lord sent a miraculous storm, followed by a miraculous calm. He then prepared a miraculous fish to swallow the runaway. In the second chapter, God miraculously preserved Jonah in the belly of the fish. He then miraculously directed the fish to vomit Jonah onto dry ground. In chapter three, the Sovereign Lord sent a miraculous revival, probably the most outstanding spiritual awakening in human history.

In the fourth chapter, we will consider the greatest miracle of all—Jonah himself! This man caused more trouble for God than did the whole pagan city of Nineveh. He was a real "yo-yo" believer, up and down, but mostly down!

A. An Evangelist Who Did Not Want Revival

"But Jonah was greatly displeased and became angry" (4:1).

In chapter three, a remarkable story developed on a foreign mission field. Israel's most formidable foe had experienced a tremendous outpouring of God's blessing. Undoubtedly, everyone was rejoicing in the aftermath of this great victory, everyone, that is, except poor Jonah. He blatantly rejected and repudiated the goodness of God to the Ninevites.

The opening word of chapter four, *"but,"* points out the contrast between God's compassion and Jonah's displeasure, and between God's turning *from* His anger and Jonah's turning *to* his anger. The final chapter is one of the most difficult passages in the entire Bible. Why, after such unbelievable blessing, would Jonah plunge into personal defeat? The prophet simply could not rejoice in the blessings of God. Imagine an evangelist being exceedingly displeased with several hundred thousand converts! Instead of being humbly grateful, Jonah was grumbly hateful. What was his problem? Was he angry because he thought God might be cruel to the Ninevites? Not exactly! On the contrary, Jonah blamed God for being too gracious and compassionate. He used these attributes of God as his reason for fleeing to Tarshish. When God offered Nineveh the same salvation He had given to Jonah and the Jews, the prejudiced preacher became angry.

The Pouting Prophet

"He prayed to the Lord, 'O Lord, is this not what I said when I was still at home? That is why I was so quick to flee to Tarshish. I knew that you are a gracious and compassionate God, slow to anger and abounding in love, a God who relents from sending calamity. Now, O Lord, take away my life, for it is better for me to die than to live.' But the Lord replied, 'Have you any right to be angry?' " (4:2-4).

In his "pouter's prayer," Jonah claimed that the Lord had made a fool of him. Before he ever set sail for Tarshish, he feared that the Lord might forgive this wicked enemy city. Now he accused God of making him look bad. Actually, Jonah did a good job of looking bad all by himself, without any help from God.

Instead of rejoicing that the Sovereign Lord of the universe had changed His mind about destroying Nineveh, this Jew grew angry with God for withholding judgment from the much-hated Assyrians. In childish self-pity he felt betrayed because his message of warning had not been carried out. How considerate of Jonah to offer himself as a spiritual advisor to God! If God had inflicted greater punishment on Nineveh than He did on Sodom and Gomorrah, the evangelist would have been greatly pleased. Shades of Tarshish! Jonah knew the heart of God, but God did not control Jonah's heart.

Discouragement turned to despondency. Since he could not have his own way, and he could not control the circumstances, Jonah prayed for God to kill him. (At this point I am tempted to say, "Go ahead, Lord; grant him his wish!" Then I remember that at times I too am much like Jonah.)

God countered Jonah's whining with a gracious question, "Have you any right to be angry?" Did Jonah have any right to be mad at the One who had given him eternal life, delivered him from his rebellion, and provided him with a fruitful field of service? God had blessed exceedingly abundantly, and His grace was the only reason Jonah was alive. Jonah, who had been the recipient of so much of God's compassion, simply had no compassion for the people of Nineveh.

Making Excuses for Jonah

What was Jonah's problem? Perhaps he was still suffering a hangover—physically, mentally and spiritually—from his recent nightmarish experience of three days and three nights on a foam-blubber mattress. Perhaps deep down in his heart he yearned to be in Tarshish, his Nineveh experience being only skin-deep. Certainly he was still clinging to his prejudicial idea that the Heavenly Father was the exclusive property of the Jews. He objected to God extending mercy to the Gentiles. True, his problems were of his own making, but they were real.

Physical Hardships

Jonah's nerve-wracking excursion was followed by the pressure of preaching an unpopular message to a pagan nation. Some of Jonah's erratic behavior might be blamed on his physical condition (which could have been avoided). Physical problems often contribute to spiritual failures.

Mental Stress

Jonah was beset with the awful sin of racial and national prejudice. Israel's God had spared a nation which might later bring defeat to them, so Jonah had developed a harsh, bitter attitude. Such deplorable attitudes are common today, and believers are not exempt from them. Racial hatred, denominational pride, even bitterness over sporting events, bring great distress to God's churches. A pastor once sternly warned me not even to mention the football game played the previous day by the two leading state schools for fear that the losing fans would angrily leave the church. What tragic sin! What misplaced values!

Spiritual Depression

Jonah was obviously more interested in politics than in God's redemptive work. In the United States today, political fanaticism so often takes precedence over spiritual concerns. What an indictment on American church-goers! If we ever get as excited about King Jesus as we do about presidential and congressional candidates, we will be rejoicing in the midst of a glorious Spirit-inspired revival.

Back to Tarshish?

"Jonah went out and sat down at a place east of the city. There he made himself a shelter, sat in its shade and waited to see what would happen to the city" (4:5).

Did Jonah ever consider the possibility of a trip back to

Tarshish? In our allegory, we need to consider this option. Is it possible to leave Nineveh and go all the way back to the disappointing place more than two thousand miles away? Unlike salvation, being filled with the Spirit is not a once-for-all experience. While we cannot lose God's eternal life, we can lose our power, blessing, and victory. However, I am convinced that most believers who have truly experienced Jesus as Lord do not return to the carnal life of Tarshish. The more common tendency is just to drift outside the city limits of Nineveh to the suburbs. (This is the reason for the many references to *downtown Nineveh.*)

A Ringside Seat for the Fireworks

Jonah did not embark on that long trip back to Tarshish to flee again from the presence of the Lord. He merely moved a short distance outside the city of God's will, built himself a booth, then sat like a vulture waiting to see if God might change His mind and destroy the city. Overtly, the degree of sin might not seem as bad in the suburbs as in Tarshish, but Jonah was just as much out of the will of God as he was during his Tarshish days. So near, and yet so far away!

In our three-city analogy, every genuine believer living in Tarshish would have at first received Jesus as Lord, the only way to get saved. Salvation is by grace through faith, but I cannot find Scriptural support for the common idea that a person can take Jesus as Savior without receiving Him as Lord: *"He became the source of eternal salvation for all who obey him" (Hebrews 5:9).* Neither can I find biblical support for the idea that we can live anyway we desire simply because we are saved by grace. That is "salvation by *disgrace!*" A genuine grace experience changes our attitudes and desires: *"For the grace of God that brings salvation has appeared to all men. It teaches us to say 'No' to ungodliness and worldly passions, and to live self-controlled, upright and godly lives in this present age" (Titus 2:11-12).*

The apostle James tells of two kinds of faith: living and dead. The difference betweeen the two is the matter of obedience and disobedience: *"What good is it, my brothers, if a man claims to have faith but has no deeds? Can such faith save him?...But someone will say, 'You have faith; I have deeds.' Show me your faith without deeds, and I will show you my faith by what I do. You believe that there is one God. Good! Even the demons believe that—and shudder" (James 2:14, 18, 19).* Salvation calls for more than a simple, "I believe."

The Lord also made His claims clear: *"If you love me, you will obey what I command...Whoever has my commands and obeys them, he is the one who loves me. He who loves me will be loved by my Father, and I too will love him and show myself to him...If anyone loves me, he will obey my teaching. My Father will love him, and we will come to him and make our home with him. He who does not love me will not obey my teaching. These words you hear are not my own; they belong to the Father who sent me" (John 14:15, 21, 23).* It is easy to see that the Lord demands an obedient faith. What pleasure would any preacher get out of lowering Christ's standards and deceiving his listeners by telling them that obedient faith is an option? Mental assent, just grunting a "yes" to salvation, is certainly not all that is required.

Saved or Lost?

For purposes of this study, we have assumed that all who are living in either Tarshish, Nineveh, or the suburbs, are genuine born-again, blood-bought children of God, saved by His matchless grace. In real life, unfortunately, this is not true. It is possible, even likely, that church members who are committed to Tarshish-living, *and are not bothered by it*, have never been truly saved. In one of the saddest passages in the Bible, the Lord describes the dire consequences on the Day of Judgment for church people who have never been born again: *"Many will say to me on that day, 'Lord, Lord, did we not prophesy in your name, and in your name drive out demons and perform many miracles?' Then will I tell them plainly, 'I never knew you. Away from me, you evil-doers!'"* (Matthew 7:22-23).

True believers living away from the Lord can expect to be continually "nagged" by their Heavenly Father until they make a total commitment to Jesus. Though He isn't harsh or mean, He chastens His children because He loves them and doesn't want them to settle for a second-rate kind of lowlife. While lost pretenders may get away with sinfulness in this life, sidetracked believers can expect "heavenly love spankings" until they repent. The loving Heavenly Father purposely makes his children miserable until they return to the fold, or until they die.

This week I talked to a heartbroken mother whose sixteen-year-old son is living in the prodigal's pigpen (located in Tarshish.) She told how, for many years before he got hooked on drugs, he loved and served the Lord. Her question was, "Do you think he might be a true believer?" My answer to her was that only time would tell. If this boy is a genuine Christian, his Heavenly Father will not sit idly by, twiddling his thumbs, while His son wrecks his life. When we are saved by God's grace, we are given *eternal* or *everlasting* life, even though we don't deserve it. God promises unconditionally that we are saved *forever.* (If He had promised us life for ten years, do you think He would take it away in five?) So, if this boy was truly saved by grace through faith, he still has the everlasting life God promised him.

However, this unspeakable gift does not give us any right to presume on God. He hates our sin. The slogan, "Once saved; always saved," is dangerous, because it is usually used by those wanting a life of sin, followed by a righteous heaven. Nowhere in the Bible is grace portrayed as license to sin.

Anytime a Christian sins, God springs into action to bring about repentance and restoration. These are the things that the sixteen-year-old boy can expect if he is a true child of God:

First, the Father will speak to him. He may use a still small voice in the night, or He may use a loudmouth preacher. If the guilty one repents, he is instantly restored.

Secondly, if there is no repentance, God spanks in love. He does not desire to hurt His children, but He desires restoration. The spankings can be severe, but once the Father sees repentance, the discipline stops. Why would He go on spanking after He gets the desired results?

Next, if there is no repentance, God takes a very scary step. He turns His child over to his own way: "I'm taking hands off you. I'm going to let you have what you want until it wrecks you." He did this with His own nation: *"But my people would not listen to me; Israel would not submit to me. So I gave them over to their stubborn hearts to follow their own devices" (Psalm 81:11-12)*. If you have ever been subjected to this third step, or if you have watched someone else go through it, you know that words can't describe the misery and torment involved. As soon as there is repentance, the Father delights to bring His child back.

Finally, if there is still no repentance, God says: "My child, I love you too much to let you go on disgracing my Name and misrepresenting My Son. I have to remove you from the earthly scene." The unrepentent one dies physically, so that he can live forever spiritually, courtesy of grace! Several New Testament passages refer to this premature physical death. A man in the church at Corinth was living illicitly with his father's wife: *"Hand this man over to Satan, so that the sinful nature may be destroyed and his spirit saved on the day of the Lord" (I Corinthians 5:5)*. Corinthian believers were abusing the Lord's Supper by not dealing properly with their sins: *"That is why many among you are weak and sick, and a number of you have fallen asleep* (died physically)" *(I Corinthians 11:30)*. The apostle John wrote: *"There is a sin that leads to death. I am not saying that he* (a brother) *should pray about that" (I John 5:16)*.

While Christians in sin face these terrible love-disciplines, non-Christians are free from them. They store up eternal punishment in hell. From what I have observed about my teenager friend I expect his mother to see her son set free shortly, either with a joyous homecoming, or with a sad, premature funeral.

A Two-Pronged Salvation?

It is quite common for believers to testify, "I took Jesus as my Savior because I was not told about receiving Him as Lord. Do you think I am really saved?" Of course, I am not the Judge, but it seems that, if sincere people admit their sinfulness, then receive Jesus by grace for all they know Him to be, the Father would delight to save them, in spite of inadequate instructions. However, it has been my observation that in such cases the loving Lord always confronts these believers with whale-like crises, forcing them to acknowledge Jesus as Lord.

Over and over we hear the testimony, "I took Jesus as my Savior when I was young, but the experience didn't mean anything to me until many years later." The Bible certainly doesn't teach such a two-pronged salvation. Jesus is to be received as both Lord and Savior at the instant of conversion. Only faulty teaching is to blame for the existing confusion. Biblically-based salvation calls for much more than just accepting a Savior to take us to heaven someday! The teaching of Lordship stands out on every page of the Scriptures, so God wants *all* His children to march under this banner.

O Glorious Day!

This old world will climax with a thrilling acknowledgement from everyone who has ever lived that Jesus is Lord: *"Therefore God exalted him to the highest place and gave him the name that is above every name, that at the name of Jesus every knee should bow, in heaven and on earth and under the earth, and every tongue confess that Jesus Christ is Lord, to the glory of God the Father" (Philippians 2:9-11).* The issue is not *whether* you will acknowledge Jesus as the Sovereign Lord of the universe; it's just a matter of *when* you do it. For rejecters, it will be too late to claim eternal life. For believers, we should be practicing now for this great occasion by giving Jesus His deserved place of preeminence.

Precious Memories in the Miserable Suburbs

In many ways a Christian's life can be even more wretched while backsliding in the suburbs of Nineveh than in the total self-life of Tarshish. Once we have tasted the delightful life of the Lord, remembering the joy of our Spirit-filled days adds a new dimension of wretchedness to life in the suburbs.

Rebellious believers in Tarshish usually have a different spiritual outlook than do backsliders in the suburbs. Having deliberately chosen Tarshish, they have never committed to the Lordship of Jesus, nor have they ever tasted of the practical aspects of the Spirit-filled life. They like living there because they want their own way, even in worship. They exercise self-rule, and they don't want to be bumped from the throne of their own heart by the Lord Jesus. They surely want to see God first thing after they die, but they don't want any interference from heaven while they are alive.

Suburbanites, on the other hand, would have already experienced some exciting and practical Christian victory before moving outside the city limits. Unlike Jonah, most of them probably never intended to backslide. They just drifted away when they took their eyes off the Lord. Not always rebellious, they can look as good as ever on the outside. Many might still be active participants in the familiar church programs, perhaps not even realizing that the glory has departed from their lives. They still know the church language, they can sing all the hymns, and they can go through through the motions of prayer. But when spiritual reality sets in, so do the doldrums of despair. Nothing is worse than having to pretend that all is well, knowing that intimate fellowship with Jesus is a thing of the past.

When the Preacher Picked on Me

My most glorious days in downtown Nineveh were spent as an English-language pastor in Taiwan. The Lord poured out His blessing and power in real revival. Almost every member was involved in personal Bible study and also in sharing the faith with others. Hundreds were reached in their homes, on the air base, in school, wherever believers went! Spiritual victories could be explained only by, "God did it." We were exposed to Heaven-sent, Holy Spirit-inspired, spiritual awakening, and for several years I rode the crest of those revival waves. What a life!

When Uncle Sam closed our military bases in Taiwan, we reluctantly returned home. Ministry in the USA was different. Even in the best of churches, I did not see those same signs of revival victory. Without realizing it, I drifted from downtown Nineveh to the outskirts of the city, yearning for the revival-fires I had experienced in Taiwan.

My new pastorate in Florida was beset with longstanding problems. What happened spontaneously in Taiwan was not taking place, no matter how loud I yelled when I preached.

Each week I met with a pastor friend who was experiencing even greater ministry disappointments than I. Each week we would "cry in each other's coffee" about our plights. My memories of Nineveh (Taiwan) made my suburban ministry in Florida even harder to take. Personal attitudes that had disappeared in Taiwan—discouragement, disappointment, despair, impatience—became a part of my life again.

One day my friend phoned excitedly, "Lew, I've been listening to a series of taped sermons that I believe contain the answer to everything that is ailing you. The preacher is obviously Spirit-filled, preaching in the power and love of the Holy Spirit. I'd like to share the tapes with you, but you must promise to listen to the entire series of eighteen messages."

How I regretted making that promise! Nothing can be tougher on a preacher, sitting in the suburbs of Nineveh, listening to *himself* preaching eighteen long messages from downtown Nineveh, sermons preached during the glory days in Taiwan. (My friend had borrowed the tapes from my secretary.)

Imagine hearing and sensing revival joy in a Christ-controlled preacher, knowing that it used to be *me*! No victory exists in the life of a "has-been." The Lord used the humiliation of listening to my own preaching to move me back downtown. A rededication based on I John 1:9 did it!

God's deliverance provides complete restoration and fellowship with Him: "*If we confess our sins, he is faithful and just and will forgive us our sins and purify us from all unrighteouness*" (*I John 1:9*). "*Confess*" means "*to agree with*" or "*to say the same thing about.*" We confess our sins when we feel the same about them as God does, when we hate them as He does. Because He is faithful and just, while we have been unfaithful and unjust, He forgives us and cleanses us. Confession got this preacher back on track.

Two Kinds of Forgiveness

We need to distinguish between judicial forgiveness (in God's court) and paternal forgiveness (in God's family). Judicial forgiveness settles the matter of eternal salvation. When we receive Jesus as Lord and Savior, the Heavenly Father promises that He will never again charge us with our sin, for He has already punished His Son with the Hell that our sin deserved. We're born again! We're in God's family to stay! We rejoice in an eternal salvation! We're assured that we are Heaven-bound! All because of this once-for-all judicial cleansing! *"In him* [Christ] *we have redemption through his blood, the forgiveness of sins, in accordance with the riches of God's grace" (Ephesians 1:7).*

Paternal forgiveness, however, is the basis for maintaining daily fellowship with God. It is the kind of forgiveness referred to in I John 1:9. This verse makes no reference to our eternal salvation. This forgiveness provides continual restoration from the daily sins which break our family fellowship with God. As we continually confess our sins (as often as we commit them), our fellowship and joy are instantly restored. We stand clean before our Father. This paternal forgiveness is the kind that takes us from the suburbs back to the center of town. Since our daily sins don't cause us to lose our *eternal* salvation, we need only to have our walk with the Lord restored. When He cleanses and forgives us, we are once again ready to worship and serve the One who *"washed us in His own blood."* Such rededication in the suburbs is amazingly effective.

Rededications do work in the suburbs, but they are a futile exercise in Tarshish. The need there is for *dedication*, bowing low before the King of Kings and yielding to Him in total commitment. How sad to watch well-meaning Tarshish-dwellers try to get right through "rededications," especially in evangelistic meetings. So many times the results don't last even until the visiting evangelist gets out of town. They are no substitute for the crowning of Jesus as Lord.

Can a Christian Commit Suicide?

In the despair and hopelessness of suburban-living, Jonah developed suicidal tendencies. Arguments abound as to whether a true Christian can commit suicide. The answer? Never while in downtown Nineveh! However, outside the city, whether in Tarshish or in the suburbs, suicide is always a distinct possibility. Believers cannot be trusted to think straight when living on their own, outside the mind of Christ. Suicide may at times seem like the best way out of the despair of a selfish life.

B. A Graduate Degree for a Slow Learner

When did Jonah finally come to his spiritual senses? Though he had learned a little aboard the ship, and a lot aboard the fish, he obviously needed further instruction.

We learn so slowly about real living and pay so dearly for our "pigheadedness." Fortunately, the God of grace and glory never gives up on His children, so Jonah found himself taking three tough advanced courses, each a painful object lesson.

Object Lesson #1: His Own Air Conditioner

"Then Lord God provided a vine and made it grow up over Jonah to give shade for his head to ease his discomfort, and Jonah was very happy about the vine" (4:6).

This vine, believed to be a fast-growing, wide-spreading gourd, was God's replacement for a booth which Jonah had tried to build for his own comfort. God provided the gourd to serve as Jonah's air-conditioning system, and it worked! The wide leaves of the gourd kept the sun off his (bald?) head, and Jonah was *exceedingly glad*, for the first and only time in the whole book!

What twisted values we exhibit when we are outside God's will! Jonah was far more concerned for his own personal comfort than for the welfare of eternal souls. When he could have been delightfully worshiping the God of Glory, the prophet was worshiping a gourd. Full of anger and self-pity because God would not destroy a million people, he was now a happy camper because he had shade. What perversion! Unfortunately, this attitude is common among believers today. We aren't interested in serving the Lord if it means leaving our comfort zone.

When Our Possessions Possess Us

"God richly provides us with everything for our enjoyment" (I Timothy 6:17). He gladly sent Jonah a gourd of comfort, but the gourd became a god. When things begin to possess us and become idols, God topples them. He insists that our confidence be in Him, not in self or money or things. C. S. Lewis summed up true riches so well: "He who has God and many other things has no more than he who has God alone." When good things become idols, misery sets in. Jesus said: *"Watch out! Be on your guard against all kinds of greed; a man's life does not consist in the abundance of his possessions" (Luke 12:15).* Jonah's air conditioner got him in deep trouble.

Object Lesson #2:
When A Worm Ate A God!

"But at dawn the next day God provided a worm, which chewed the vine so that it withered" (4:7).

While God is in the pleasures of life, He is also in the thunderstorms and rains. He is in the judgments as well as the pleasures. He is involved in our losses as well as our gains. "He *brings prosperity and creates disaster" (Isaiah 45:7).* Jonah's second object lesson involved a worm with a calling from God—to break the air-conditioner. The worm was obedient (remember, only men and demons disobey God), and Jonah's happiness toppled with every crunchy bite. The obedient worm got a delicious meal, and the disobedient prophet got another painful lesson. We can almost hear Jonah pathetically crying "Why me?"

Object Lesson #3:
"Boy, It's Hotter than a Whale's Belly"

"When the sun rose, God provided a scorching east wind, and the sun blazed on Jonah's head so that he grew faint. He wanted to die; and said, 'It would be better for me to die than to live.' But God said to Jonah, 'Do you have a right to be angry about the vine?' 'I do,' he said. 'I am angry enough to die' " (4:8-9).

A sultry wind provided a heavy trial, burning everything in sight, including poor Jonah's head. The scorching east wind left him comfortless and faint. Gone were his earthly joys and his sense of security and well-being. He expressed his anger about the destroyed air conditioner. This loss of personal pleasure brought on another death wish. Slowly and sadly Jonah was coming to the end of himself.

Jonah's reaction is common among selfish people when God doesn't do things their way. It is called "biblical thumbsucking."—"I'm having a pity party. I can't go on. This is not the way I planned things" When our marriages, our children, our jobs, or our churches are not exactly what we prayed for, we get angry with God and give up. "I'd just as soon die." In the process we usually blame God for the problems, rather than realizing that sin has been the culprit.

In spite of his grumbling, Jonah's latest conversation with God seems to have brought his woes to a conclusion. He might finally be shaping up!

A Tale of Three Cities

Warped Values

"But the Lord said, 'You have been concerned about the vine, though you did not tend it or make it grow. It sprang up overnight and died overnight. But Nineveh has more than a hundred twenty thousand people who cannot tell their right hand from their left, and many cattle as well. Should I not be concerned about that great city?" (4:10-11).

The gourd was nothing, but it had become Jonah's life. Just as destruction of the gourd brought sorrow to Jonah, destruction of Nineveh would have brought sorrow to God. The contrast between the two events caused the Lord to question Jonah about his right to be angry. God showed Jonah how confused his thinking had been, valuing a plant, but disdaining a whole nation of people. The gourd had lasted only a day and a night, and Jonah had nothing to do with creating it or sustaining it. If the loss of a vine hurt Jonah so deeply, shouldn't God feel even greater compassion for a thousand year old city? He had created these people for His own pleasure, then watched as they walked away from Him, mad with sin and drunk with evil.

The Lord rebuked Jonah for his twisted values. How could a man show no concern for dying people who faced an endless eternity apart from God? Nineveh was the world's largest city: *"But Nineveh has more than a hundred and twenty thousand people who cannot tell their right hand from their left, and many cattle as well"* (4:10). (Some scholars think that this refers to *women drivers*!) More likely it refers to children or perhaps to those who do not know the spiritual difference between their right and left hand, those who are unable to make moral judgments. Even the reference to *many cattle* contained a measure of rebuke. Certainly Jonah belabored his grief over the gourd to an excessive degree. Were not even the cattle more important than a plant? John Calvin said, "If Jonah was right in grieving over one withered shrub, it would surely be a harder and more cruel thing for so many innocent animals to perish."

God was saying, "Jonah, since the day you bought your ticket to Tarshish, I have been trying to get you to see things as I do. I spared you over and over and gave you new opportunities, yet you remain unwilling to give Nineveh one chance. You must get your priorities and values in order." From the first verse to the last verse of this book, God was interested in one thing—the obedience of His servant.

The God who charted a course for Jonah has a similar plan for each of our lives. Our rebellion may have us sitting out in the middle of the Mediterranean in a storm, or in a fish's belly, but as long as we are alive and breathing, the Sovereign Lord will hold on to us in order to accomplish His purpose.

God sent a fish to preserve Jonah. He sent a gourd to shake him from his resentment. He sent a worm to shatter his confidence in earthly things. Finally, He sent the wind to silence him from every controversy with his Heavenly Father. At long last Jonah's selfishness seemed to be silenced as he beheld the sovereign love and power of his God.

The Lord wants from us the same submissive spirit he demanded of Jonah. First, He wants us to see the whole world as He does, recognizing lost friends (or even enemies) as victims of Satan and sin. Secondly, He desires for us to be available so He can express His Calvary love through us. Thirdly, God desires for us to be a sign to our generation, showing that the Christ who lives in us is truly the answer to this world's needs.

We do not know what finally happened to Jonah. It seems likely that he eventually learned the most significant truth in all of life—the sovereign greatness and glory of the Lord!

CHAPTER FIVE

PERSONAL EXPERIENCES IN NINEVEH

Regretfully, I could tell you more than I want to about my life in the suburbs. Just as Paul described suburban living in the seventh chapter of Romans, I could write about entirely too many similar experiences when I've cried out: *"What a wretched man I am! Who will rescue me from this body of death?"(Romans 7:24).* Paul's answer is great: *"The law of the Spirit of life set me free from the law of sin and death" (Romans 8:2).* What a life the Lord Jesus offers us!

A few years ago, my ten-year-old grandson accompanied me on a preaching assignment to a neighboring state. On the trip home, Digger (last name Graves!) asked me to share some of my ministry experiences with him. For several hours we talked about amazing things the Lord had brought about in this old-timer's ministry, many of them events which took place before Digger was born. As we rode along, he kept saying, "Gramps, tell me another story." What fun to share "downtown Nineveh" experiences with this great guy!

To emphasize the kind of spiritual thrills we can expect from the Lord, I want to "tell you another story," or maybe several!

A. Evangelism in Nineveh

Sad to say, I've played the kind of evangelistic games that seem to have filled our churches with people who have not been saved. I even played the "number's racket" which has captivated so many churches and pastors. At the close of a long ministry, the memory of such endeavors leaves me cold and ashamed. What a difference when the Lord empowers us to use His methods of sharing the Gospel with lost friends!

Chief of Sinners

While in seminary I took a week off to go to Jefferson City, Missouri. I preached a revival meeting at the "Goat Hill Baptist Church" (really "Parkview," but the old-timers called it "Goat Hill"). The pastor had a deep love and concern for the lower economic folk at Parkview.

On the opening night, a lady welcomed me by saying, "Don't let the pastor talk you into visiting my husband Art. He's a hard man. I've seen how he treats evangelists." After the service, Art's daughter also urged me to avoid her dad's harsh treatment.

These two dear women were quite convincing. I was determined not to visit Art. However, preachers have to come across as "spiritual," so the next afternoon when the pastor asked if I would like to visit Art, I lied piously and uttered a sanctified, "Yes."

All the way to Art's house the butterflies flew out of formation in my tummy. I prayed that Art wouldn't be home, but God apparently didn't hear my prayer. My heart sank when I saw this rough-looking, unshaven, uncombed sixty-three year old ogre. I was both disappointed and scared when he invited us in.

As we sat in the drab little living room, the pastor turned the whole situation over to me. Attempting a courageous stance (on the outside), this coward mumbled, "Art, are you a Christian?" Instead of an uncivil reply, he simply answered, "No." Then I heard myself asking, "Has anyone ever told you how to become a believer?" His "no" response puzzled me, because I had heard about dozens of preachers who had visited him through the years. My cowardly boldness suddenly increased as I requested ten minutes to share the Gospel message with him. I was dumbfounded when he said, "Please do!"

In simple fashion I explained to him how the sinless Savior had taken all of Art's sins into His body, and how God the Father had punished Jesus for those sins. I then

A Tale of Three Cities

planned to tell Art of the eternal punishment his sin would bring if he did not trust in Christ's atoning sacrifice, but Art stopped me in my tracks. Within ten minutes of our arrival, big tears streamed down his dirty face, and he fell to his knees. I'll never forget his prayer: "God, this preacher tells me that You can save me from all my sin. If You can, go ahead and do it!" Of course, Art was immediately saved.

This fifteen-minute visit dazzled my mind. The next day the pastor of the First Baptist Church congratulated me for reaching the hardest sinner in town. What an evangelist I was! The truth is that I was little more than a spectator to the saving grace of God. This had been an obvious encounter between Art and the Lord Jesus. I could take no credit at all.

About an hour later, as I arrived for the evening service, I heard everyone outside buzzing nervously about Art being in the church building. Upon entering I was amazed at how a man's appearance could change so drastically in an hour. When I finished preaching, a hush fell over the crowd as this clean-shaven, nicely-dressed man walked down the aisle and publicly acknowledged his new-found salvation. What a preacher Art had become in a couple hours! He challenged the entire church: "I see a lot of young people here tonight. Don't make the same mistake I did. I've wasted sixty-three years in sin. Today I learned that God forgives wicked sinners and gives us new life!" What a fantastic conversion!

Exactly one year later I returned to Goat Hill for another meeting. Art wasn't there. I couldn't pretend not to be disappointed—apparently another flashy profession without Holy Spirit possession. For a year I had rejoiced in Art's life-transformation. Now I wondered if it was "for real." I had seen others fizzle in the faith, but somehow I had expected better from Art.

After the service, Art's wife handed me a letter. Written from the tuberculosis sanitarium in St. Louis, Art expressed deep regret that he couldn't be with us. He assured me of his deep love for the Lord Jesus and related how he had led four fellow patients to a saving faith in Christ.

A week after I returned to seminary, I received a letter informing me of Art's death. He didn't get much time to experience life in downtown Nineveh, but two Hell-deserving sinners are going to enjoy a tremendous forever with our Lord Jesus when I see him again!

What a difference between genuine conversion brought about by the Holy Spirit and the anemic attempts of man to get people to "make decisions."

Religious but Lost

At the other end of the spectrum from down-and-out Art, I met two long-time preachers with no true convictions. Many religious failures are not those Christians living in Tarshish or the suburbs, but church members with no spiritual life at all, dead in trespasses and sins. In the Sermon on the Mount, Jesus said: *"Not everyone who says to me, 'Lord, Lord,' will enter the kingdom of heaven, but only he who does the will of my Father who is in heaven. Many will say to me on that day, 'Lord, Lord, did we not prophesy in your name, and in your name drive out demons and perform many miracles?' Then I will tell them plainly, 'I never knew you. Away from me, you evildoers'"* *(Matthew 7:21-23).*

A Tale of Three Cities

The year before I became a Christian, I hitch-hiked each weekend from Scott Air Base in Illinois to visit relatives in Indiana. Even though I claimed to be an atheist, I faithfully attended services at the local Congregational church. The sermons were boring, but I couldn't understand why my two old Welsh friends, Evan and Dick, kept giving the pastor such a hard time. At least he wasn't long-winded! (I can hear a lot of ugly remarks coming my way!) What difference did it make what the old man preached?

I was stupefied though when "the Rev" asked me to preach for him one Sunday in February. I knew absolutely nothing about the Bible, and I was petrified to speak publicly. When I told the pastor that I was not a believer, he suggested that I preach something appropriate for Lincoln's birthday! Fortunately for everyone, I refused to begin my preaching career at that time.

To most people's satisfaction, the pastor finally retired after serving fifty-seven years in the ministry. Two years after leaving Indiana, he returned to apologize to his adversaries, Evan and Dick. After a lifetime of meaningless religious service, this man finally came to understand what it meant to be "born again," and he experienced salvation during his retirement years. Shortly after this I also became a Christian. When Jesus became real to me, I understood why Evan and Dick, both converted during the famous Welsh revival, had begged the pastor for years to preach the Word. I also understood that the poor man couldn't preach something he knew nothing about. He might just as well have preached about Abraham Lincoln!

Religion is such a curse! It's wonderful that the pastor

finally experienced a personal relationship with the Lord Jesus. But how sad that a fifty-seven year ministry would be so useless! So many well-intentioned church members attended Sunday after Sunday without ever hearing him preach the life-transforming truth about the Lord Jesus!

I came across a similar situation during a Bible Conference in Kansas City a few years ago. After I had preached for several nights about the Lordship of Jesus Christ, a man addressed the congregation, "I have been a Baptist preacher for thirty-five years, but until now I never realized that Jesus wanted to be the Boss of my life. I've used all of the terms and much of the Scripture that we've heard this week, but I never applied the Lordship of Jesus to my life in practical ways. I can truly rejoice now, for I have turned my life over to Him in total commitment. I'm already experiencing the Christian life with new vision and excitement, but it can't change the fact that I lost my family and my ministry while I lived in the defeat of the carnal life."

Rejecting the Giver of the Gift

Perhaps the greatest earthly feature of my Christian life is the kind of people who have become my friends. I am convinced that friends, not money, constitute true Christian riches and make life meaningful. I have never been famous, nor have I ever known many famous people. After cheering fanatically for the New York Yankees for sixty-six years, I must admit that I've never known any Yankees personally. (The closest I've come was to be good friends with Bobby Richardson's missionary aunt!)

A Tale of Three Cities

I haven't known many famous Christians either. One notable exception was a close friend, the renowned Prince of Preachers, Dr. R. G. Lee. My wife Joanna and I had warm fellowship with Dr. Lee and his beloved Lady Lee. I still have a number of his handwritten letters, each one telling me that he prayed for me every day.

I never understood why Dr. Lee and I had such a close friendship. He was quite dignified and cultured, while I was lacking in both of those graces. Dr. Lee was a warm and gracious man, but one afternoon I saw him in a completely different light. While he was leading our new, small church in a revival crusade, he asked me to take him to a men's clothing store so he could buy a suit. I hesitated, because Dr. Lee was at that time the only man in America who wore double-breasted suits. When I suggested going to a tailor, he replied, "Silly, I'm not interested in a suit for me. I want to buy one for you."

Immediately I refused. I was needlessly concerned about the size of the love offering that our church would give this world-famous preacher. I didn't know if the honorarium would be enough to buy a suit. When I turned him down, he immediately became quite angry. I received an unforgettable rebuke, "Young man, you have done a terrible thing to me. You have rejected me. When you refuse a gift, you are not rejecting the gift itself, but rather the giver of the gift." Then his scolding became theological in nature, "Don't you realize that when lost people reject the gift of eternal life, they are not merely refusing salvation. They are rejecting the Almighty God Himself, the Giver of the gift?"

I tried to reverse my decision, but Dr. Lee stalked off to

his hotel room. I dreaded going to pick him up that evening, but when I met him, he was as charming and cheerful as ever, and we remained close friends. What an important lesson that grand old man taught me. Salvation is referred to as a gift ninety-two times in the New Testament, but when we turn it down we are not rejecting salvation. We are rejecting God Himself!

I never got the suit. A week after the meeting concluded, the mailman brought a nice letter from Dr. Lee, with a $50 gift for Joanna and $5 for each of our kids. I got nothing except the lesson about rejecting the giver! Though I may have spurned Dr. Lee, this experience caused me to rejoice that I had not turned down the God of all grace when He offered me eternal life through Jesus Christ our Lord.

B. Spiritual Spectaculars in Nineveh

Since the Christian life is empowered by the Holy Spirit, we believers ought to be living in a supernatural realm. Our lives should be characterized by happenings which can be explained only by "God did it!" Churches likewise should be experiencing continual victories that no lodge or club could possibly duplicate. Both individual believers and churches should be exercising full control over the devil and all the forces of evil. This is our heritage in Christ.

"Come Out of This Man, You Evil Spirit"

One evening in Taiwan a "hippie-type" visitor and his female companion attempted to disturb our worship service. While talking with the young man it was rather easy to discern that he was demon-possessed. He reacted to the Scriptures in a violent manner, and I admit that I was petrified. Then something wonderful happened! The man grabbed my Bible and slung it across the auditorium yelling, "Can't we have an intelligent discussion without using that Book?"

This was all I needed. My confidence in the Lord and in the Bible grew to amazing proportions. I was no longer fearful. I realized that the demons were scared of both my Lord and His powerful Word!

I will spare you the details and take you to the climax of this encounter. I had never dealt with demons, so my only hope was to follow examples set forth in the Word. Relying entirely on the authority of the Lord Jesus, I commanded in His Name that the evil spirits depart and return to the pit from which they came. Only trouble is that nothing happened! The guy grabbed his girl, they ran out of the building, and I never saw them again.

I was devastated. The two Air Force pilots who had witnessed the entire scene went home with me. We studied all night about what went wrong. Even with no previous experience, we felt that we had done everything in tune with God's Word. Why hadn't the man been set free?

We have a good God! Two weeks later one of the pilots and his fiancee were walking on a side street in the huge city of Taipei, a hundred miles from our home. Just *by luck* they ran into the couple who had fled from our meeting. The man apologized for not contacting us. He related that the demons left him later that night, and he had turned to the Lord Jesus as his Savior. He and his companion were planning marriage and a return to the United States. He had already turned himself in to the authorities to settle a criminal charge. Wasn't it *lucky* that these two couples ran into each other on a back street of a very large city?

Incidentally, there are two kinds of luck that I don't believe in, good and bad! What we call "luck" is really Divine providence: *"The lot is cast into the lap, but its every decision is from the Lord" (Proverbs 16:33).*

Why the delay before the demons left the man? I am afraid this might have been God's way to humble me. While I know that I personally am no match for any demons, I might have been overcome with pride in casting them out. Instead I went home fully aware of my own inadequacy. Then our gracious God later showed me that *"I can do everything through him who gives me strength" (Philippians 4:13).*

In the years that have passed since that scary event, I've had several opportunities to deal with demons. I do not consider myself to be an exorcist, but I do believe that every child of God has the power and authority of the Lord to overcome all Satanic forces: *"You, dear children, are from God and have overcome them, because the one who is in you is greater than the one who is in the world" (I John 4:4).* But let me emphasize again, this works only in downtown Nineveh! Don't try to cast out demons while you are in Tarshish or even in the suburbs!

We believers should be giving the devil a real hard time.

In fact, every Christian should be a devil-chaser: *"Submit yourselves, then, to God. Resist the devil, and he will flee from you" (James 4:7).*

Touched by an Angel

In 1989, the Foreign Mission Board sent me to Hong Kong to conduct a Bible Conference. On my way home I visited Taiwan, where we had lived for four years. Only those who have been in that country can understand my poor timing—Chinese New Year! This holiday celebration is unparalleled in our country. I couldn't get a train ticket to Taichung, our old home, so I stayed at the Baptist compound and celebrated with seven million people in Taipei.

Procrastination caused a problem on the last day of my visit. I had to find some gifts for my family, but I didn't know my way around Taipei, and I was still suffering from my utter failure to learn the Chinese language twenty years before. Time was also a consideration, for I was scheduled to preach to the missionaries that night.

Jeanette, a two-year mission volunteer, came to my rescue, or so I thought! She wrote the address of the Baptist compound in Chinese characters for me. We then took a cab to the shopping center, then she continued on to her church. I completed my shopping, caught a cab, and handed that address to the driver (who could speak no English.) About an hour later this perplexed driver, who had stopped several times to ask directions, just shook his head. A look at the meter convinced me to get out. The poor driver was as lost as his poor passenger, who admittedly has absolutely no sense of direction. I had no idea if I was thirty feet or thirty miles from my destination.

I took the written address into a camera shop, but the clerk was unable to help me. He went outside with me to a small alley, where we asked a delivery man for assistance. He also had trouble deciphering the strange characters. As the three of us stood in the alley, an attractive Chinese girl crossed the road and came toward us. I was quite surprised when she asked if she could be of help, for there was no way she could have known that any of us had a problem. When we showed her the address, she said she would take me there, even though she also seemed perplexed about the address. I confess that I suspected she might be a woman-of-the-street, so I argued that I did not want her to spend the holiday helping me. She insisted, however, and shocked me when she paid my bus fare. We made at least five transfers before I got the brilliant idea of calling a missionary at the Baptist compound who could give her directions. At the pay phone I accidentally dropped all my coins onto the sidewalk. Three young children grabbed them and ran into a department store. My benefactor took out after them, soon returning with my money and asking me to please forgive the children.

My phone calls to several missionaries went unanswered, so the young lady said, "Let's go this way." In a few minutes I noticed the tall Baptist building. We made it!

This trip took more than three hours. During our afternoon together I tried several times to share the Gospel message with this kind friend, but she showed no interest in learning about salvation. I tried to pay her, but she turned down my money. I asked for her address so I could send her a gift, but she would not give it to me. Her only request was that I show my gratitude to her by serving others. In all our time together I realized that I hadn't even learned her name.

My servant-friend accompanied me just inside the walled compound. The guard at the gate laughed when we showed him the address we had been trying to use. Apparently Jeanette's Chinese-writing was on the same par with my Chinese-speaking! How we even got close was a mystery.

As we stood in the courtyard, the young lady told me that she had really enjoyed her holiday afternoon. I still had a strong desire to share with her about the Lord Jesus, but each time I tried, she seemed to hide behind the language barrier. As she was leaving, I asked her to wait until I could find a missionary who could tell her about Christ's atoning work. Again she showed no interest. We said goodbye, and I watched as she joyfully skipped down the sidewalk and out the gate.

Please do not read any further unless you believe in the supernatural.

Are Not Angels Ministering Spirits?

As my friend went out the gate, I saw a missionary friend coming in. I ran to the gate, about ten yards away. In those few seconds, she was gone! Vanished! There was no place she could hide. She disappeared in the same fashion that she first appeared, out of nowhere! And I made it to my preaching engagement just in time.

Before you make arrangements to have me committed, let me quote from the New Testament: *"Are not all angels ministering spirits, sent to serve those who will inherit salvation?" (Hebrews 1:14).* As a reminder, angels do inhabit human bodies, but they do not need salvation as humans do!

Did I say that this happened in downtown Taipei? I'm sorry. I should have said downtown Nineveh!

Divine Healing

I was taught in seminary that Jesus says, "I don't do healing anymore." But when two new converts appeared at our home in Taiwan for a late-night visit and asked, "Pastor, does James 5:14-15 still work?" it was difficult to say, "No, that part of the New Testament is obsolete."

I have problems with most "faith-healers," not only because of their methods, but also because I believe God has assigned the gift of healing to "the elders of the church" (James 5:14). So when these two young military men asked, "Are you an elder?" I accepted an extremely hard assignment.

John said, "Larry has a problem. (Names changed.) He learned today that he has a venereal disease (which he had contracted before he became a Christian, and thought was cured). It's in a stage which will destroy his nervous system, then take his life. It's the worst case the doctors have ever seen. Can the Lord heal him?"

Ordinarily I would have a lot of reservations about dealing with such a case. I always have to pray as did the sick boy's father: *"I do believe; help me overcome my unbelief" (Mark 9:24).* Somehow, though, perhaps because of the naive faith of my visitors, I was inclined to believe that the Lord would do the impossible.

A Tale of Three Cities

The three of us had a very simple service. We confessed our sins, we prayed, and we anointed Larry with oil. (All three of us Baptists discovered that even Baptists can have anointing services!)

Though it's not very sanctimonious, I must tell you about the oil we used. My family was planning to move in a few days. The olive oil that I always kept on hand for such an occasion (but had never used) was packed in a crate. I spied a can of "Three-in-One Oil" on a shelf and immediately thought "Trinity Oil!" Since the oil is merely a symbol of the Holy Spirit, the "Trinity Oil" proved to be most effective.

Larry called me three days later, reporting that his atheist doctor was baffled because he couldn't find a trace of the disease. When Larry shared with him about the Lord's healing, the doctor said, "Son, you have a lot of religious hangups," to which Larry responded, "But I don't have the disease, do I, Doc?"

Larry had been told by the doctors that he would never be able to return to his home in America, that he would eventually lose his mind, and then die a horrible death. The last letter I received from him told about how he is serving as a Baptist deacon in a southern city, and it included a picture of his wife and five sons. Perhaps the day of divine healing is over, but please don't tell Larry.

I don't understand everything about healing. It's impossible to figure why some believers get healed while other equally dedicated believers do not. It's difficult to know just how and where faith fits in. I am not a healer, but I rejoice in some exciting times in which the Lord has blessed my ministry with healing miracles, including visible infirmities that have been completely cured. What a shame that so many churches never trust the Great Physician for any miracles! Incidentally, the Great Physician's clinic is located in downtown Nineveh.

C. Laughter in Nineveh

The best place for joy and laughter is downtown Nineveh. I have nothing but pity for Christians in Tarshish, and I don't even appreciate my own life when it takes me to the suburbs. Life is full of "spiritual fun" when my mail is addressed to downtown Nineveh.

Oswald Sanders, a famous missionary leader, was once asked by a young missionary volunteer what he considered to be the most important trait that a foreign missionary should have. His brilliant answer was, "A sense of humor, especially the ability to laugh at yourself." (Everybody else laughs at you, so you might as well get in on the act!)

My Florida church once invited my four adult kids back for a service in my honor. In testifying, my kids avoided the horror stories of being preacher's kids and growing up in parsonages. Instead, all four remarked about the fun and laughter we had in our home. This may help to account for the fact that years later, all are walking with the Lord and serving Him faithfully.

I shall never forget the hilarious times of laughter I've had with dear friends like Jack Hopkins, Gene Sanders, and Tom

Higgins, all of whom are now doing their laughing in heaven. We had a lot of very serious discussions and experiences, but I shall never forget the great spiritual contribution of laughter that they brought to my life. I consider myself to be a very wealthy man because of friends like these, and many others.

Wilfred and Lou Richardson have been choice friends. After their son became a Christian during our Taiwan ministry, this couple trusted the Lord in St. Charles, Missouri, while listening to tapes of our services. In the next few years, about thirty of their relatives were saved.

When we left Taiwan, I traveled around the U.S.A. leading Bible Conferences. Since I traveled Interstate 70 in Missouri many times, the Richardsons, just four miles off the highway, provided me with a room and many delicious meals any time I was nearby.

One Friday morning I stopped on my way to a weekend meeting in Windsor, Missouri. As always, Lou had a great meal ready, this time ham. Before I left, we made arrangements for my return after the Sunday evening service. My plans were to arrive at about 2 a.m., grab a few hours sleep, then leave for home in Florida at 6 a.m. Monday. Because of the ugly times involved, we agreed that the Richardsons would not plan to see me.

Before I left for Windsor, Lou prepared a brown paper sack for me, which, of course, contained two ham sandwiches, a good snack for my trip. When I arrived at the home where I was staying, my hostess said, "We have a ham in the refrigerator. Would you like a sandwich before the service." I politely declined, but after the service, she got out the ham and fixed a snack. She also told me to raid the refrigerator and help myself to a ham sandwich at any time. The next day I skipped breakfast, but at noon the pastor took me to lunch at a member's home. You guessed it—ham sandwiches! Back at my quarters, before the Saturday meeting, my hostess again offered me a ham sandwich, which I again politely refused. After that service, however, we sat down again to a nice snack. Only one option on the menu—ham! The Sunday noon meal was at a farmhouse, and the hostess outdid herself in preparation for it. The table looked like a typical Thanksgiving spread, with one notable exception—no turkey. Instead, a beautiful country ham, all decked out with pineapple, cherries, and other elegant trimmings, occupied the center spot.

I packed my car on Sunday afternoon so I could leave immediately after the evening service. After declining my hostess' offer of a pre-church ham sandwich, I drove off that night in the direction of the Richardson's, a brown paper sack at my side. About midnight I got brave enough to open it, and I was just hungry enough to partake of both ham sandwiches.

Arriving back at the Richardson's about 2 a. m., I found a note on the table: "Help yourself to the ham in the refrigerator. I also packed a lunch for your trip to Florida. Love, Lou."

We were too poor to throw good food away, although I admit to being sorely tempted. Early afternoon, somewhere in Indiana, on my way to Florida, I prayed for the Lord to bless my lunch and to provide me with the courage to eat it! Nothing like a couple ham sandwiches to cheer a weary traveler.

I didn't have the nerve to tell Lou about this for several years, but one night, when she was present in a St. Louis meeting, I confessed the whole ham ordeal to the entire congregation. What does this have to do with life in Nineveh? Nothing! It simply shows the kind of fun I've had for the past fifty years of ministry. Certainly the Christian life is not all fun. We are called to sacrifice and suffer, even when we are in the center of the Lord's will. However, there is also a superabundant amount of laughter available, with lots of fun times. I'm sure I have laughed far more than the average person, especially those in Tarshish who really have nothing to laugh at.

D. Unusual Happenings in Nineveh

If I were to list the most influential Christians in my life, the name of Dr. Curtis Vaughan would be near the top. This faithful seminary professor imparted to me the most exciting and helpful theological truths I've ever learned. He "caused my God to grow much bigger" by introducing me to the Bible doctrines of grace—the sovereignty of God, election, predestination, and other much-abused, much-neglected truths. These teachings changed my man-centered thinking into God-centered theology. I am quite certain that I could not have lasted in the ministry, had it not been for the great God-honoring doctrines I learned in Dr. Vaughan's classes on Romans and Ephesians.

When I became a pastor, I invited Dr. Vaughan for annual

Bible conferences. We developed a good friendship, but as the years passed, I left the country, and we rarely saw each other.

One day, after I had become a pastor in Florida, I was unable to put Dr. Vaughan out of my mind. From early morning through the afternoon I couldn't stop thinking about him, even though I had not seen him or talked to him for several years. When I went home that afternoon, my wife suggested that I call him. I was reluctant to do so. We never phoned each other, and I didn't know what I'd say. Finally, to get some peace of mind, I gave in and called his home.

When Dr. Vaughan came to the phone, I heard a great deal of commotion in the background. He said, "Lew, I'm so glad you called. Let me go to my study so I can hear you better."

I halfway apologized, explaining that I didn't know why I was calling. Dr. Vaughan responded with surprise, "You've got to be kidding. You honestly don't know why you're calling me?" He then told me that his wife had died several days before, and he had just returned from her funeral service. His house was full of friends who had come to support him, but Dr. Vaughan admitted that he was yearning to hear from former students (who, like I, had no knowledge of his loss.) Dr. Vaughan told me that he was convinced the Lord had directed my call to fill a void in his life at that very time.

Ten years later, a friend and I visited Dr. Vaughan at the seminary. He told my friend how the phone call had enriched his life, claiming that it was one of the most unusual blessings he had ever received. I'm grateful that the Sovereign Lord overruled my reluctance to call. At just the right time He put me in touch with the man who had first taught me about His sovereignty.

Why shouldn't we expect unusual happenings, the kind which cannot be explained in natural ways, to be commonplace in the Holy Spirit-controlled climate of downtown Nineveh?

E. Family Life in Nineveh

How sad that most churches miss out on spectacular activity even though the Bible clearly declares the supernatural as a way of life for New Testament believers. What impact could be made on believers and unbelievers alike, if we relied on Holy Spirit power to bring about unexplainable phenomena.

At the same time we must recognize that some people get hopelessly carried away in a craze for only the supernatural. They often neglect the down-to-earth, dynamic Holy Spirit-control of everyday matters. As much as we might be impressed with the miraculous, a stronger testimony might be what the Lord can do in the daily practical matters, such as marriage and family life.

Til Death Do Us Part

A survey in the late sixties by Campus Crusade for Christ acknowledged the well-known fact that one of every three marriages in our country ends in divorce. This extensive survey revealed, however, that this sad statistic changed to one out of every 1,015 marriages collapsing when both partners honored the Lord by obeying the teachings in the fifth chapter of Ephesians about family life. What an advertisement for the genuine Christian life!

Kids Deserve a Nineveh Upbringing

A few years ago while teaching at a Bible conference I was treated to a delicious meal in a lavish home. The kind hostess boasted that her four children had all made straight A's throughout their school lives, all had doctor's degrees, and each was making a six-figure salary. I felt so inadequate. My four kids had received a good share of A's (although I regard grades as a very poor measure of anyone's worth), and if I added their salaries *together* it might also total six figures, but not one doctor's degree in sight! Raising four "failures" left me with no bragging material!

As our conversation turned to spiritual matters, this fine lady's eyes filled with tears. She said sadly, "I regret that not one of my children is walking with the Lord." Suddenly I felt very wealthy. After all, what good are straight A's, big salaries, and doctor's degrees on the road to eternal Hell? I am glad to have two preacher sons and two faithful daughters who are walking with the Lord, actively serving Him, and furnishing me with the twelve best grandkids ever invented! Think of it! I possess the wonderful gift of a whole family ready for the Rapture, every last member bound for Heaven. I utterly reject the politicians' talk that "Education is the answer." The real answer is total commitment to our Creator and Redeemer.

The wealth of my Christian family is a stirring testimony to my wife Joanna. Not only has she been a faithful companion for forty-six years, but she has been an unusually wonderful mother, and she's even a pretty good grandma! I'm so glad I didn't marry in Tarshish!

I have borrowed a prayer for my grandkids from the mother of Count Zinzendorf, the dedicated Reformation leader. She prayed, "May the Father of mercies rule the heart of this child, so that he may walk honestly and uprightly. May sin never rule over him, and may his feet be steadfast in the Word; then he will be happy for time and eternity." Kids deserve the privilege of being raised in downtown Nineveh and educated at the University of Nineveh.

F. Financial Freedom in Nineveh

One of the outstanding delights about life in downtown Nineveh is that our Lord chooses to sponsor us financially. While the Bible never promises financial riches, our Father's will is that we be financially free, never worrying about money matters. Biblical principles, usually the direct opposite of the world's financial schemes, are guaranteed to bring refreshing freedom.

I could write a lengthy book about the Lord's provision for my family, beginning in 1979, when I learned some liberating principles from Larry Burkett, the financial expert. Before that time I could testify only about bondage. I must admit that I have never owned any large sums of money. An examination of my slim bank accounts and other assets would cause nightmares for most financial advisors. The Lord's provision, however, has been nothing short of miraculous.

The folowing accounts do not advocate carelessness about saving, either for emergencies or for retirement. I relate them only to remind us of the admonition: *"Command those who are rich in this present world not to be arrogant nor to put their hope in wealth, which is so uncertain, but to put their hope in God, who richly provides us with everything for our enjoyment"* *(I Timothy 6:17).*

Who Wants To Be a Millionaire?

Early in my Christian life I met Virgil Wagner, an outstanding star in the Canadian Football League. Virgil and Mary had become believers while in Canada. We became good friends when they returned to their home in Illinois. We enjoyed studying God's Word together until I left to enroll in Bible College. While Virgil tried his hand at selling cars, I became a student and a paper boy.

Existing at near-poverty level, Joanna and I were driven to prayer when our refrigerator contained only a pound of hamburger, a bottle of water, and no milk for our baby son. Payday was still a week away, and we had agreed never to ask anyone except the Lord for financial help. The same day that we prayed about our plight, we received a letter from the Wagner's. Though we had not heard from them since we left Illinois, there was no message, just a twenty dollar bill that changed my whole life!

When we returned home I shared with our church what a blessing this gift had been. Virgil then stood up and completed the testimony. He explained how, when he had sold his first car, he and Mary prayed about donating the commission to the Lord's work. While they were praying about whether to send it to Billy Graham, World Vision, or Youth for Christ, the Lord impressed them to send $20 to their very needy friends at Bible college. Isn't that just like the Lord to be so concerned about an insignificant young couple?

That relatively small contribution changed my life and set the stage for many future financial miracles of greater dimensions. Truly our God is alive, alert, available, and adequate: *"For the Lord God is a sun and shield; the Lord bestows favor and honor; no good thing does he withhold from those whose walk is blameless" (Psalm 84:11).*

I have discovered that the world's best financial institutions are located in downtown Nineveh.

A Birthday Present from Heaven!

My favorite financial story took place at the time of my daughter Margaret's eleventh birthday. I was still three years away from learning the life-changing principles of financial freedom. Although I made an adequate salary, we lived in constant financial bondage. Two money demands were facing me on Wednesday: Margaret's birthday present, and a $250 payment to Uncle Sam. We had no money for either. To further complicate matters, I was scheduled to leave for a Bible conference early Wednesday morning.

In typical "suburban" fashion, I devised a scheme, even though it nauseated me. After my Tuesday night Bible study, I planned to visit our treasurer and ask for a $300 salary advance. Joanna could then pay Uncle Sam and get a present for Margaret. What a great suburban solution! Unfortunately, it was wrapped around Tarshish-like thinking, so the Lord over-ruled it.

That evening a first-time visitor attended our study. Afterward, as I hurriedly prepared to leave for the treasurer's home, I heard a knock at the office door. My heart sank when I saw our visitor Joe standing there. I really didn't have time for him.

His question annoyed me, "Pastor, how are your finances?" After all, a pastor must have some dignity, and my financial problems were none of this stranger's business. In my suburban-like response, I lied and said, "Everything's fine," so Joe left.

Immediately the indwelling Holy Spirit started nagging me. I confessed my sin to my Heavenly Father. So full of pride that I lied to the man whom God obviously had sent to help me. What a rotten sinner! Thanks to Calvary, I received instant forgiveness. I knew I would also have to apologize to Joe, but not now! I had to get to the treasurer's house.

Just then I heard another knock. Joe again! He said, "Pastor, I was leaving the parking lot, but I felt impressed to come back and ask again about your finances." I then told him that, having already confessed my lying and pride to God, I also wanted his forgiveness. I told him of my plan to get a salary advance. He handed me a roll of bills and asked, "Would this help?" My ecclesiastical dignity left me. I grabbed the money and counted it right on the spot. Needless to say, it was exactly $300!

I thanked Joe and shared with him how mightily the Lord had used him in my behalf. Then I politely asked him to excuse me so I could get to K-Mart before closing time. I had a birthday present to buy. Joe objected and said, "Follow me to my house."

My new friend explained that he had just moved from Ft. Lauderdale. He had just closed his jewelry business and wanted me to look at some items that were left from his closeout sale. When I saw the price tags, I suspected that I was going to be swindled, but this "angel from God" said, "I'm not selling you anything. I'm giving you whatever you choose for your daughter." My eyes popped when he suggested a 14K gold ring with the word "love" carved among the diamond chips, and a $250 sale tag dangling from it. Think of it! I had never seen this man before that evening.

When I arrived home I finally persuaded Joanna to awaken Margaret. Imagine those eye-popping gals when they saw that piece of jewelry, with the price tag which I "forgot" to remove. My wife thought she was married to a bank-robber. When she asked, "Where did you get that?" I was able to answer truthfully, "God gave it to us."

What adds another dimension to this story is that, while I remained friends with Joe until his death some twenty years later, he never gave me another gift. The Lord had used him for that one occasion when we needed special love. Such is life in downtown Nineveh!

Saving for a Rainy Day?

Through the years it was exciting to watch our Heavenly Father faithfully provide for us in unusual and amazing ways. It was always hand-to-mouth (His hand to our mouth) and nothing much left over. While life had been a series of financial miracles, we were getting to the end of the road with almost no material assets. Reaching age sixty-three with a meager bank account, no retirement program, and no real estate, would cause old-age panic in Tarshish. In Nineveh, however, such conditions merely give the Lord the opportunity to provide for His children. We were not able to "save for a rainy day," so why would the Lord send one?

Early in my Christian life I learned a thrilling lesson from my father-in-law, Dr. Eugene T. Pratt. This well-educated, dedicated man of God never made a large salary, and a medical condition prohibited him from getting more than $5,000 life insurance.

Dr. Pratt's lifetime ambition to be a seminary professor was realized when he was called to be Professor of Evangelism at Southwestern Baptist Seminary in Fort Worth, Texas. After serving a few years in that capacity, however, he realized that his heart was really in his former ministry as Director of Evangelism in Missouri. When that position opened again in January, 1965, he was glad to return to it.

At that very time, the Executive Director for Missouri Baptists was arranging for a new insurance program for the State leaders. The new group policy was to exclude Dr. Pratt and one other uninsurable man, but the Director insisted that these two be included or he would not accept the program.

On April 1, 1965, Dr. Pratt had a new $25,000 policy. One month earlier he had purchased a new house, a new car, and various appliances, securing mortgage insurance on each item. On April 18, 1965, Dr. Pratt suffered a massive coronary attack and died.

While we're still not over the loss of this great man, we can rejoice that God provided so faithfully for Mrs. Pratt. If Dr. Pratt had died two months earlier, his estate would have been valued at $5,000, hardly enough for a rainy day. As wonderful as this blessing was for Mrs. Pratt, the lessons learned probably meant even more to me. I have never known a more faithful minister. However, he could hardly have qualified as a financial success, and he certainly wasn't prepared for "a rainy day." All that this giving man had going for him was the Lord Jesus and a good number of Bible promises. I learned quite a few valuable lessons as I saw the Lord provide for him.

The Bible furnishes financial precepts that the Wall Street Journal never thought about. Jesus is not only the Lord, Savior, Great High Priest, and Great Physician, but He is also the world's best Financial Advisor.

I forgot to mention that the Pratt's home was located in downtown Nineveh!

No Good Thing Will He Withhold!

I was convinced as a young Christian that we should never make our financial needs known to friends or relatives—just to the Lord Himself. As a result, the Lord continually carried on unusual works in our behalf. Certainly His provision for our senior years is a fit illustration as to how He operates.

Dennis Richardson was a close friend ever since his conversion in Taiwan. Now, many years later, while Joanna and I were sleeping soundly, the Lord began waking Dennis, burdening him about getting a house for us. In order to get some sleep, the poor guy finally agreed to do what he could to help. The only problem was that he lacked the necessary funds to buy us a house.

At our summer camp, Dennis was overjoyed to learn that God was also working on some other men concerning the house. What a relief when friends from Indiana and Iowa approached him about this matter. He wasn't going to have to fund the whole project by himself.

Dennis contacted Lloyd Hansen, a director of "Lord of Life Ministry," a small corporation established to support my Bible conference ministry. He discovered that the Board members had also been concerned about our housing. It seems the Lord was working on men all over the country, and we knew nothing about it! These men put their resources together and presented us with a gift of $55,000 (which was $48,000 more than we had ever had at any one time.)

Within a week Bill Judge, a Board member, asked us to look at a house in Kissimmee, Florida. I really questioned Bill's judgment. The house was up for sale for $300,000, and I had "saved" only $55,000.

Bill explained that the owner had offered the property to a local church for a $200,000 tax write-off, plus $100,000 cash. The church had turned down the offer. The Lord impressed Bill to call the owner to see if he would consider selling it to Lord of Life Ministry. The owner not only agreed, he voluntarily lowered the cash price to $80,000. Without any appeals being made, friends around the country sent the amount still owed. The last $10,000 came from a friend in Texas, another "Taiwan veteran," whom we had not seen for several years. Without knowing about the house, or that the balance owed was exactly $10,000, he sent a check for $10,002. (God always does *"immeasurably more than all we ask or imagine, according to his power that is at work within us" (Ephesians. 3:20).*

Imagine the adjustment we had to make to our "rainy day situation!" After living in modest houses all our lives, we had to learn how to live with a swimming pool, a six-car garage (we're four cars short!), two electric dishwashers, and a beautiful chandelier (which neither of us can play!). We honestly never even desired this kind of luxury. We remain amazed at His provision, but after forty years, it's hard to be surprised anymore. The apostle explained our situation so well: "And *my God will meet all your needs according to his glorious riches in Christ Jesus" (Philippians 4:19).*

The house is located in a beautiful section of downtown Nineveh.

I could share so many other financial experiences and miracles, but this should be enough to show what kind of a God we serve. Giving us a house is one of the *smallest* things He has done. His most precious provisions are all *invisible!*

So end the ramblings of an old preacher, Forgive me, I always swore when I was young that I would never be like those old preachers who bore everyone with stories from the past. I am convinced though that every Christian should be enjoying Nineveh experiences just like the ones I've related. As my life draws to a close, I realize more and more what a poor, weak, undeserving believer I am, but wow! What a Lord I have!

CHAPTER SIX

THE UNWRITTEN LAST CHAPTER

The Book of Jonah ends very abruptly and has no conclusion. It ends with God speaking. He always speaks the last word, in Jonah's life, in our lives, and in human history. The world always has been, and always will be, under His control. No mere human being will ever thwart His purpose. The theme of obedience is the very point that God was continually emphasizing to Jonah. The outstanding truth that grew out of Jonah's experiences was that "Salvation comes from the Lord."

Did Jonah ever come around? I believe the unwritten fifth chapter would reveal that he finally did come to understand the heart of God. Apparently he sat down under the inspiration of the Holy Spirit to write about his life so that he could help others. Who else could have been used so effectively to pass on this great story for our edification?

Downtown Nineveh!

Victorious living requires every believer to reside in the heart of Nineveh, not in Tarshish, not even in the surrounding suburbs. This is an either/or decision; it cannot be both. We cannot choose a little bit of Nineveh and a little bit of Tarshish, or a little bit of downtown with some suburban living thrown in. No ruler has ever demanded more of his subjects than does Jesus: *"Any of you who does not give up everything he has cannot be my disciple" (Luke 14:33).* He *demands* to be Lord, and He *deserves* to be!

Accepting a Savior or Receiving the Lord?

Is there a valid biblical basis for offering Jesus as Savior (something He does) without insisting that He be acknowledged as Lord (who He is)? Is it fair for us to tell people about the promise of heaven someday without also advising them of the Jesus Principle of Life? I think not.

Lordship is the dominant theme of the Bible (434 New Testament references). It results in both godly living and victorious death. How sad that we have put the emphasis on the Saviorhood of Jesus (24 New Testament references), as though Christianity were merely a religion to die by. Too often our churches are filled with people who, even *if* they are prepared to die, are doomed to despair while living. What ever happened to the *abundant life* that Jesus promised?

What are the practical results of Jesus' death and return to life? Many true answers can be given: "to save us from our sins," "to forgive and cleanse us," "to dwell in us," "to take us to heaven." However, the clearly stated purpose for His death, burial, and resurrection is that He might be our Lord: *"For this very reason, Christ died and returned to life so that he might be Lord of both the dead and the living" (Romans 14:9).*

If I Should Wake before I Die

Jesus was not crucified just to be a ticket to heaven for self-servers, or just to be an insurance policy against eternal hell. Certainly He is our only deliverance, the only way to a blissful eternity with the Heavenly Father. But the main thrust of the scriptures is not merely getting to heaven some day. We are to let the Christ of heaven live in us today and experience a little bit of heaven on the way to heaven.

Our evangelistic approach usually centers around the issue, "What if you died tonight?" Although this is a valid question, an equally valid one is, "What if you do not die tonight? Can Jesus as Lord do anything to enrich your life *now?*" If you should die tonight, you desperately need Jesus Christ as your Lord and Savior. He *said, "I am the way and the truth and the life. No one comes to the Father except through me" (John 14:6).* However, if you do not die tonight, you will be living tomorrow, and you just as desperately need Jesus Christ as your Lord and Savior. He is as essential for successful Christian living as He is for successful Christian dying. Jesus Christ is not a luxury for our lives. He is the Absolute Necessity!

Seeker-Sensitive Services

A number of churches have been conducting services in which they attempt to appeal to visitors by removing anything that would be offensive to lost sinners. Good as this sounds, we do no favor to lost friends by taking away the "offense of the Cross," for without this emphasis, it is impossible for anyone to be truly saved.

"Seeker-sensitive services" do seem to build large attendances, but even this term doesn't seem to square with the scriptures. In describing lost people, Paul said: *"As it is written: 'There is no one righteous, not even one; there is no one who understands, no one seeks after God' " (Romans 3:10)*. Lost people often seek after religion, they seek to soothe their guilty consciences, and they seek nice things from God, but the scriptures are clear: *"There is none that seek after God; no, not one."* A lost person wants His own way *(Isaiah 53:6,)* so he does not want to bow down to God in submission.

Every service should be "Seeker-sensitive," but "Seeker" must have a capital "S". The matchless grace of God that separates Christianity from all other religions has an amazing feature, God always does the seeking! "For the Son of Man came to seek and to save what was lost" (Luke 19:10).

Our churches' greatest need today is not to develop "Seeker Services," "user-friendly messages," or contemporary services which appeal to worldlings. None of these innovations can adequately replace a good old-fashioned service in which we "Bring Forth the Royal Diadem and

The Unwritten Last Chapter

Crown Him Lord of All." We miss out on so much when we bring the world's ways into our fellowship, just to try to apease the lost. I like to sing some modern choruses, but I recognize that "Seven/Eleven" ditties (singing the same seven words eleven times) is never going to replace great old hymns about the Cross of Calvary. We do not do a service to anyone when we quit singing time-tested songs that present the saving Gospel of the Lord Jesus.

What modern chorus can compare with my favorite, written two centuries ago by Frederick Whitfield? It's not just that I'm an old man who doesn't like modern things, but it's a matter of substance. Consider what these words would mean to that sinner friend who is in desperate need of regeneration:

> I saw the cross of Jesus, When burdened with my sin;
> I sought the cross of Jesus, to give me peace within;
> I brought my soul to Jesus, He cleansed it in His blood;
> And in the cross of Jesus I found my peace with God.
>
> I love the cross of Jesus, It tells me what I am—
> A vile and guilty creature, Saved only through the Lamb;
> No righteousness nor merit, No beauty can I plead;
> Yet in the cross I glory, My title there I read.
>
> I trust the cross of Jesus, In every trying hour,
> My sure and certain refuge, My never failing tower;
> In every fear and conflict, I more than conqueror am;
> Living, I'm safe, or dying, Thro' Christ, the risen Lamb.

Safe in the cross of Jesus! There let my weary heart
Still rest in peace unshaken, Till with Him, ne'er to part
And then in strains of glory, I'll sing His wondrous power
Where sin can never enter, And death is known no more.

It's more than just being an "old fogey" that makes me thrill to that hymn! It won't hurt any of my "mod" grandkids, or their friends, to worship with such a hymn of grace. (I'd want it sung at my funeral, if I had either the time or the inclination to attend! I'm afraid I'll be busy with other things.).

Our great need is to bow low before Jesus and acknowledge Him both as Sovereign King over all creation and as Lord of our individual lives. This procedure involves giving Him the only thing He ever asked for, our bodies as living sacrifices. *"Therefore, I urge you brothers, in view of God's mercy, to offer* [the Greek verb calls for a one time, once-for-all transaction!] *your bodies as living sacrifices, holy and pleasing to God—this is your spiritual act of worship. Do not conform any longer to the pattern of this world, but be transformed by the renewing of your mind. Then you will be able to test and approve what God's will is—his good, pleasing and perfect will" (Romans 12:1-2).* Such a Coronation Service allows God to move us from Tarshish to Nineveh, right into His heart!

Our Assignment: Preaching Jesus as Lord

Just as God gave Jonah directions about his ministry in Nineveh, He also has assigned ministry to each of us. While the specifics involved in the different ministries will vary,

The Unwritten Last Chapter

the general assignment is the same for all. The apostle has revealed this two-fold assignment, guaranteeing successful results if we are obedient: *"For we do not preach ourselves, but Jesus Christ as Lord, and ourselves as your servants for Jesus' sake" (II Corinthians 4:5)*

First, Paul defines our message. We are to preach Jesus Christ *as Lord.* Sadly, we have substituted preaching on the Savior with an emphasis on dying rather than bringing the prescribed message on living. It's great to know how to die in grace, but our disobedience in preaching has brought a loss of spiritual vitality. We can have good funerals, but there isn't much sign of revival!

Then Paul describes our service to others. We are to be *"servants for Jesus' sake."* No looking out for the "Big I," because we are to *"consider others better than ourselves,...and to look out for the interests of others" (Philippians 2:3, 4).* If I truly believe this, I will regard myself as the least important member of my church. Can you imagine being part of a fellowship in which each member (including the pastor, elders, and deacons) considers self to be the least important person, living to serve everyone else? This is exactly what God designed for New Testament churches. Believers must not push themselves for fame, money, or a place of honor, because *"he died for all, that those who live should no longer live for themselves but for him who died for them and was raised again." (II Corinthians 5:15).*

This God-given ministry is His only plan for reaching a lost and dying world. When we carry out our assignment, God promises to turn on the lights that Satan has turned out.

We can ill-afford to substitute our own plans and programs for one that has God's approval and wisdom.

What a wonderful experience I had in 1983, centered around the *"preaching of Jesus Christ as Lord."*

While flying to a convention, I was seated next to a seventy-year-old Roman Catholic nun, fully dressed in the old-style traditional habit. At takeoff, I began to read my Bible. The sister asked, "What book are you reading?"

A little surprised that she didn't know, I answered, "The Bible."

"Oh, I know it's the Bible," she said rather disgustedly, "but what book of the Bible are you reading?"

As our flight continued, this nun asked me if I had ever been born again, the only stranger who ever cared enough to ask me about my soul. Next she questioned me about my church affiliation. When I told her I was Baptist, she caught me totally off-guard. If her desire had been to ridicule my denomination, she couldn't have come up with a more painful, penetrating question. "May I assume then," she asked, "that you know Jesus as Savior, but not as Lord?" Perhaps I should have been angry, but after preaching in hundreds of Baptist and other evangelical churches through the years, I was aware that the sister was being insightful, not mean and nasty. For decades I have recognized that many churches, especially those in pursuit of big memberships, were offering "cheap grace" instead of obedient faith. After assuring my new friend of my stand on the Lordship issue, she shared the story of her conversion, which had occurred twenty years before.

Having served faithfully as a nun for twenty-five years,

The Unwritten Last Chapter

this religious worker was intrigued by a "revival" sign in a school yard. Not knowing what went on in such a meeting, and being unfamiliar with the evangelical way, she took her seat on the second row, before noticing that enlightened evangelicals always sit in the back. Not wanting to create a scene, she decided to stay where she was. That night she heard, for the first time, a powerful sermon on the reality of Jesus.

After the sermon the preacher extended an altar call, requesting those who wanted Jesus as Savior and Lord to stand. Touched by the message, she stood, then noticed that she was the only one standing! Those Baptists in the back were all glued to their seats, looking like nothing could ever move them! When the preacher then asked all who desired spiritual help to come forward, she hesitated, embarrassed about being dressed in her nun's habit. Without realizing that the Holy Spirit was working mightily in her life, she felt strangely drawn to obey the preacher's call. As she moved to the front, she "became instantly aware that Jesus had become her personal Savior and Lord." She had passed from religion to Christianity, from death unto life!

Immediately the new believer began to share her faith openly. In the next twenty years she led six priests and twenty-three nuns to a saving faith in the Lord. This ministry has caused her to remain in the Roman Catholic Church, even though she disagrees with some of the doctrines and practices. Although we have never again met, we continue our friendship each year by exchanging Christmas cards. I have found very few evangelical friends who match the sister in her enthusiasm about Jesus the Lord!

The Sister's Question: "Savior...but Not Lord?"

Was there any validity in the sister's pungent question? Was her assumption about Baptists correct? Have we been guilty of emphasizing Jesus as Savior, but neglecting the importance of His Lordship? Are we preaching a "lop-sided gospel" that emphasizes getting people into heaven while failing to teach that Jesus demands to be "Boss?" I would like to tell you that the sister was "all wet," but I must admit that I find entirely too much truth implied in her question. Perhaps we need to blush in shame about the disastrous results we have produced.

Even our denominational statistics show that something is wrong. We have no earthly idea where at least one-half of our members are. They fall into that "non- resident" or "I'm leaving town, don't bother me" category. Of the other half whom we can identify, only about one-third are involved in the ongoing programs of our churches. One-third of one-half is not much to brag about! And there isn't too much comfort in the fact that some other denominations have even more embarrassing statistics. Our insane quest for numbers has created a spiritual monster, a problem that only the Lord can straighten out. A lot of people seem to rest on a momentary "decision" to get them to heaven, a concept that is foreign to the scriptures. So many of the "decisions" don't seem to turn into lasting discipleship

Basic to all this is the question of biblical truth. Does the Bible really teach that Jesus is to be "Lord and Savior?" Does the Bible place emphasis on Jesus being "Boss" of our lives?

The Biblical Answer: "Savior and Lord"

Consider again the word count showing that, in the New Testament, "Savior" is used twenty-four times, while "Lord" is referred to some 434 times. While we can't build a theology on the number of times a word is used, we can't completely ignore it either. The fact that Jesus is the world's only Savior is an extremely important New Testament truth. He is *"the way, the truth and the life" (John 14:6)*. Peter said there was no other name by which we can be saved. (Acts 4:12). Jesus is our salvation, and that is glorious! But this wonderful Savior also demands to be Lord, and He deserves that place of preeminence.

The apostle Peter concluded his challenging sermon on the Day of Pentecost with this statement: *"Therefore let all Israel be assured of this: God has made this Jesus, whom you crucified, both Lord and Christ" (Acts 2:36)*. (We do not "*make* Jesus Lord." God has already done this! We need only to acknowledge the fact.)

Paul affirmed this same truth when he wrote: *"For this very reason, Christ died and returned to life so that he might be the Lord of both the dead and the living" (Romans 14:9)*. Consider also the oft-quoted Gospel invitation: *"That if you confess with your mouth, 'Jesus is Lord,' and believe in your heart that God raised Him from the dead, you will be saved." (Romans 10:9)*. Just "believing in Jesus" is obviously not all there is to salvation. The devil himself "believes" and even trembles because of it (*James 2:19*). The issue of being saved is more than just mental assent to Bible truths. As was true with the rich young ruler, many are willing to "believe" in order to get to heaven, but they want no part in obeying the Sovereign Lord. The scriptures do not base salvation on a wish about the after-life, going to heaven or escaping hell. We are saved by grace through faith in His finished work, but genuine salvation involves an obedient faith. *"He became the source of eternal salvation for all who obey him"* (*Hebrews 5:9*).

CONCLUSION

Let's review the analogy we have studied in "A Tale of Three Cities." First, there was Nineveh, the place to which God called Jonah; the city that represented God's will for him, the city of revival.

Next there was Tarshish, the city to which Jonah fled to escape the will of God. Tarshish represented the place of Jonah's disobedience and rebellion. For us, it's the place where Jesus is accepted as Savior but rejected as Lord, the place where we "do our own thing."

The third city was Joppa, the place of decision. This is where Jonah paid his fare to deliberately disobey the Lord. We Christians are confronted with this same choice: Nineveh, the place of spiritual victory, or Tarshish, the place of spiritual defeat.

Finally, we got even more specific by referring to *"downtown Nineveh,"* where Jesus is truly Lord. The farther we get away from downtown Nineveh, the farther we get away from the will of God and His blessing. Even living in the suburbs of Nineveh will not work. Every believer, every family, and every church faces this Lordship issue. We must decide whether or not we really want Jesus to have His rightful place of preeminence?

The Book of Jonah forces us to see our own power struggles with God. We need to examine what He has asked us to do that may have caused a contest of wills with Him. What are the challenges to our unconditional obedience to the Lord? Where are we right now, in a Tarshish of escape or a Nineveh of obedience?

As was true with His prophet Jonah, the loving Heavenly Father is committed to using all His children. Our Lord not only leads us to our Nineveh, but He gives us a continual flow of grace that enables us to live in downtown Nineveh. And Jesus, who is *"greater than Jonah,"* will never leave us alone until we come to a place of spiritual rest in Him. When we know Jesus personally; when we experience His grace, His love, and His mercy, our power base changes from *our* will to *His* will for us.

May the Lord apply these teachings very personally to each of our hearts through the Holy Spirit.

The Worst Word in the Dictionary: "Lost!"

This book's primary emphasis has been about believers who are living in either Nineveh or Tarshish. We have tended to ignore a large group who do not reside in either place. I refer to those who have no relationship with the Lord Jesus, those who are *lost.*

For one who has never been to Calvary's Cross, the

Conclusion

principles set forth in this book may be confusing, even ridiculous. The apostle Paul wrote: *"For the message of the cross is foolishness to those who are perishing, but to us who are being saved it is the power of God" (I Corinthians 1:18).* Spiritual truth will never make sense to those who have not been born again: *"The man without the Spirit does not accept the things that come from the Spirit of God, for they are foolishness to him, and he cannot understand them, because they are spiritually* discerned" *(I Corinthians 2:14).*

Saving faith is the unreserved commitment of one's life and eternal destiny to the Lord Jesus Christ. For this reason, I am not enthused about using easy formulas (steps one, two, and three) to present the Gospel. Neither am I overly excited about "Spiritual Laws" or "Roman Roads" or asking a lost sinner to "pray a prayer." The rich young ruler, in his desire to get to heaven, very likely would have nodded assent to any of these so-called plans. However, when he refused to submit to the conditions of Lordship which Jesus demanded, he went away without the salvation he had been seeking.

Salvation is God's work from beginning to end. When we are ready to repent, the Holy Spirit begins an inner work to convict us of the awfulness of our sin. He makes us aware of specific sins and gives us a consciousness of our self-centered nature. Then He creates an urgent desire in us to renounce our sinful ways.

Simultaneously, the Holy Spirit reveals how the sinless Son of God *"bore our sins in his body on the tree, so that we might die to sins and live for righteousness" (I Peter 2:24).* The apostle sums up so clearly His atoning sacrifice: *"God made him who had no sin to be sin for us, so that in him we might become the righteousness of God" (II Corinthians 5:21).* A holy God must punish sin, so the Perfect One *"became sin for us."* In those three hours of darkness, as He hung on the Cross, the Father laid on Him every agonizing feature of the lost person's eternal hell, including separation from the Father, loneliness, torment, darkness, thirst, and all the other tragic sufferings described in the Bible. He was our Sin Substitute: *"But he was pierced for our transgressions, he was crushed for our iniquities; the punishment that brought us peace was upon him, and by his wounds we are healed" (Isaiah 53:5).*

God imputed our sins to Christ's account and punished Him for them. A criminal, upon hearing this, asked me, "Are you saying that He took the bum rap for my sins?" At first I was set back by his language, then I replied, "That's exactly right. Very well put!" But there is more! Not only did God transfer our sins to Christ's account, but He also imputed Christ's righteousness to us, enabling all who receive Him to experience eternal life and holiness.

What a swap! We give God the sin that has caused all of life's problems. In exchange, He gives us the righteousness of His Son, who promises to dwell in us forever, even living life for us: *"I have been crucified with Christ and I no longer live, but Christ lives in me. The life I live in the body, I live by faith in the Son of God, who loved me and gave himself for me" (Galatians 2:20).*

Our part in salvation is to repent of sin, then receive the Lord Jesus by grace through faith. Immediately and permanently we become His children. We are born again! *"God demonstrates his own love for us in this: While we were still sinners, Christ died for us" (Romans 5:8).*

Conclusion

The commitment to Jesus Christ is two-fold: an initial decision, and a continuing process. When you believe, you enter an intimate relationship with Christ. You acknowledge His authority with a radical commitment of your life to Christ. Simply stated, becoming a Christian involves submission to Jesus Christ as Lord, with a sincere intention to be an obedient disciple.

This does not mean that at the point of initial commitment you will understand all the implications of discipleship or the rule of Christ in your life. Learning the principles of growth will be a lifelong process. At first you will have the understanding of a child, but even child-like faith can submit without any conscious reservations.

To illustrate, imagine my being hired to work in a nuclear physics plant. Be assured that I know absolutely nothing about this subject. The first day on the job I am introduced to my new boss, Mr. Jones. Certainly I couldn't build a nuclear bomb on that first day, but I can submit to Mr. Jones from the very first moment.

From that point on, my life will be a testimony as to how yielded and dedicated I am to my boss. If Mr. Jones tells me to empty the wastebasket, I do so. If he tells me to clean the windows, I do windows. If he tells me to build a bomb, I have to confess my complete dependence on Him. I must yield to his wisdom and ability, not my own. So it is with a new believer. So much about the Christian life is baffling, especially to a brand new spiritual baby. It's a long process of walking with the Lord, studying the Word, praying, and relying completely on the only One who has ever lived the Christian life successfully. A new child of God has to patiently develop such a life, but, from the moment of conversion, the new believer can pledge his love and obedience to his new boss.

The most wonderful result of true conversion is spiritual union with Jesus Christ. This union doesn't come from just "making a decision," or joining a church, or getting baptized, or doing church work. It's not just an emotional experience, nor is it merely taking a Savior so that you can go to heaven and escape the future penalty for your sin. Salvation is a commitment to the absolute rule of Jesus Christ in your life, a living relationship with your Lord and Savior, now and forever more!

Printed in the United States
1152500002B/365